WINDY WITH A CHANCE OF MURDER

A CAPE MAY MYSTERY

MILES NELSON

WORKING STIFF PRESS
www.MilesNelsonAuthor.com

Windy With a Chance of Murder

ISBN - Print - 979-8-9887472-1-5

ISBN - ebook - 979-8-9887472-2-2

Cover background photo by 37447729 Charmphoto @ Dreamstime

All other artwork and design by Miles Nelson

Thanks to Lee Burton of Ocean's Edge Editing

WORKING STIFF PRESS
www.MilesNelsonAuthor.com

 Formatted with Vellum

To Bonnie and Starla, who make life fun and interesting

1

"Okay, Tate, let's get down to it. Who do you think did it?"

"Well, sheesh, Marty, that's a pretty big question. I mean: 'Who did it?' Did which one? Or all of them? A lot went on in that house." Saxby sipped his coffee before setting the cup down and gazing into the dregs for a few moments. "But I'm glad you brought it up, because we need to talk about it. You know, at first, I thought it was all just the work of one person. Some kind of maniac maybe—I'm not sure. But now, after everything we've seen, I'm starting to think there could be more than one killer working together. Or maybe even playing off each other. That make sense to you?"

"Yeah, I think it does, actually," Banks said. "It occurred to me there could be two or more perps acting together. Could even be like some of the victims are collateral damage. But why? That's the thing. I'm not seeing a motive yet."

"Right. I'm not seeing the motive yet either," Saxby said. "Motive would probably give us the killer. The first guy was poisoned—we know that, which, as you know, tends to point to a woman, but in itself doesn't help with motive. Then you have the guy who was hit on the head with the axe. That points more to a man as the killer. More likely than not anyway."

"I agree with you again on that," Banks said. He carefully examined the slice of toast in his hand before selecting the right area to take a bite. "It's unlikely that was done by a woman. Possible, of course. A strong woman could have handled that axe. Yes, possible, but unlikely. That was the first one that was messy. Bloody, I mean."

They were interrupted when the waitress came over with a coffeepot in hand, steam curling from the top. "Sorry to interrupt, but can I top you up? Got a fresh pot of Costa Rican here for my two favorite police chiefs."

"Sure, thanks, Lexi, I won't pass that up," Saxby said. "I'll take the check when you have a minute. No hurry."

She filled his cup with the dark brew, and did the same for Chief Banks, who had nodded his assent. She set down a handful of creamers before heading back to the kitchen.

"So, we agree that it's possible there could be more than one killer..." Banks said. "Crazy as it may sound, we should also consider that there could be more than one motive. As long as we're throwing ideas at the wall."

"I like that," Saxby said. "Throwing ideas at the wall. Reminds me of a guy I knew years ago, back when I was with the state police, one of the top detectives. When we were stumped on a case and hashing out different ideas to see what made sense, he would say we were 'throwing spaghetti at the wall to see what sticks.' He was only half joking, because it was a good part of the process. I learned a lot from that guy."

He sipped at his coffee and appeared to think carefully before nodding in appreciation. "Oh yeah, this is some good stuff. Costa Rican, she said, right? I'll have to find out where to get some of this for home. So, anyway, back to motive. You're suggesting we could have six people murdered in or around this big old remote house, with some of it based on different motives. I guess. Sure. Why not? I'm open to it."

"Or, as long as we're throwing spaghetti, could be six people for six different motives," Banks said. "Get a bunch of people together in one place and then start doing them in for different reasons. Possible yes, but no, the more I think about that angle the less I think it makes any sense. Let's not get too far ahead of ourselves. The next episode comes out on Thursday, and after that there's just one more until we finally have all the answers. There's four people left on the island, and I can't wait to find out who gets it next. I might even make some popcorn for the finale."

"I hope they give us the answers," Saxby said. "You know how some of these mini-series kinda leave you hanging and you have to guess what really happened. Of course, putting it like that reminds me how real life can be that way too. As you well know, I've had a couple of cases right here in town that left some questions unanswered even after the files were officially closed. Frustrating, but you know how it goes, the powers that be and all that jazz … close the case and move on…"

"Oh yeah, I get you on that one, Tate, but try not to get too cynical," Banks said. "To say that real life doesn't always wrap things up all neat and tidy is putting it damn mildly, but that's what we've got."

The waitress returned to set the bill down on the table. Banks reached for it, but Saxby beat him to it. "Now, Marty, you know our agreement. I get the check in Cape May. You get the check in North Wildwood. Those are the rules."

"I know, but it seems like you get ripped off," Banks said, "because you've got better breakfast places over here in Cape May. Hey, whenever we meet up for dinner next time, maybe we can make it the Dragon House. You know, Wildwood is neutral territory."

"Sounds like a great idea to me," Saxby said. "I'll mention it to Angela and maybe we can get something on the calendar for next month. I'll admit I've thought of their Hunan beef more than once recently. Yeah … now you've got me looking forward to it." He set some bills down on the table and took a last sip of coffee before they grabbed their coats and headed for the door, giving a last wave to Lexi and the cook working the griddle on the way out.

At about sixty-five degrees, it was warm for early October, with a light breeze coming in from the open Atlantic across the street, and a clear blue sky. Saxby and Banks lingered on the sidewalk, breathing in the fresh sea air for a minute before Saxby's phone rang. He dug it out of a shirt pocket to answer, seeing that the call was coming from one of his deputies, Chase Connor III.

"Morning, Three. What's up?"

"Good morning, Chief," Connor said. "Are you still at George's? I called your cell because I thought you were at breakfast with Chief Banks. I thought that would be better than hitting you with the radio in a restaurant."

"All good, Three," Saxby said. "We just finished up and came outside a minute ago. What do we have going on to start this beautiful day?"

"We've got a body, Chief," Connor said. "Just off Golf Lane. You know there's that little alley that runs parallel and between Washington and Lafayette. I don't know if it even has a name, but there's a few houses back there. Lady looking for her cat this morning saw the neighbor's door open, got no answer when she knocked, looked in and found him. She's a retired nurse, so she kept her cool and called it in. Said she could see he was dead. I got here first, and Brody and two of the other guys a few minutes after. EMTs are on the way. Looks like some kind of struggle, or maybe a fight, but I guess an accident could be possible. Middle-aged man, appears healthy. I mean, you know, aside from being dead. Haven't found ID yet, but Brody thinks he might be one of those scientists who work at the lab out by the old beach club. We'll poke around."

"Damn. Okay, then. Good work, Three," Saxby said. "I'll be there in a few. Do your poking around and make sure to secure the area and keep an eye out for neighbors."

Saxby hung up the phone and put it away in a pocket after noting the time. He looked at Banks, who he could tell had heard the conversation. "Well, Marty, I made it almost to nine-thirty thinking it was going to be a beautiful day. You have time to come along, since you're already here?"

"Sure, Tate, why not. I don't know Golf Lane but I'll follow you over. Hopefully I won't regret eating a big breakfast."

2

L ess than five minutes later, the two police cruisers turned into a narrow lane from Washington Street, making a right after half a block onto an unpaved but well-maintained alley. They pulled over to the side to park against a dilapidated wooden fence that marked the rear boundary that ran along the edge of the back yard of one of the big Victorians on the main road. On foot, they continued past an ambulance and several other police cars to where the alley ended at a low brick wall. A small parking area was flanked on either side by a pair of rectangular two-story houses that were each roughly the size of a large two-car garage with an added second floor.

Deputy Connor emerged from the open doorway of the building on the right to greet Saxby and Banks as they approached.

"Chief, Chief Banks," Connor said, nodding at the new arrivals. He swept his hand across the area to indicate the two housing units, pointing to another of the big houses over on the main road. "This property we're on right now is actually part of that house there on Washington Street, so the owner of that house is the landlord for these. The lady in the other unit there—Donna Brandt is her name—found the body. She came out to call her cat and saw the door open across the way here, and went to check it out. Retired nurse and a sharp lady. She went back inside just before you came up. The dead man is just inside on the floor. First floor looks like some kind of combined lab and office, with the living area upstairs. According to Miss Brandt, his name is, sorry, was … Forbes, Lewis Forbes. Lived alone. Oh, looks like Dr. Coyle just arrived…"

Saxby and Banks turned to see the man who'd come up behind them. They recognized Doctor Mark Coyle immediately, having both known him as a friend for years, and also having worked with him in his role as county medical examiner on numerous occasions.

"Now, Tate, I think I've asked you before to please stop finding bodies when I'm here in town visiting my aunt," Dr. Coyle said, pretending to give Saxby a serious scowl.

"I know, Doc, I know," Saxby said. He and Banks both shook hands with the doctor. "I will try to remember that. Anyway, you're just in time. We just got here ourselves and were about to head inside. Marty's along for the ride because we just met up for breakfast. After you."

Inside, they were greeted by Sergeant Brody and one of the patrol officers who reported to him. "Morning, Chief, gentlemen," Brody said, nodding to the men as they came in. He gestured off to one side. "The body's right over there. A Dr. Forbes, according to the neighbor. We haven't touched him apart from the EMT guys checking out his status."

Dr. Coyle went around to the far side of a long, low counter to where a man's body lay face-down on the cement floor. He knelt down to check for a pulse at the man's neck. Next listening at several places on the man's back with a stethoscope taken from his medical bag.

"Well, he's certainly dead," Dr. Coyle said, after standing up. "That's for sure. Very cold to the touch, and that's quite a wound to the back of the head there. Somebody help me turn him over please."

"Sure thing, but just one sec," Saxby said. He looked over at Sergeant Brody. "Before we move him—Roy, did your guys get all the pictures you need?"

"Yeah, Chief, they got plenty of the body and all around the area," Brody said. "They're working on the living area upstairs now."

With that, Saxby and the doctor knelt next to the body and worked together to turn the man onto his back, revealing a damaged and bloodied face.

"Well, that's something now," Banks said. "Something pretty hard hit him in the face, too. Looks like he took quite a wallop. Maybe a couple wallops."

"You're right about that," Saxby said. "Something pretty hard hit him in the face, or his face hit something pretty hard."

They watched as Dr. Coyle took an infrared thermometer from his bag and pointed it at the man's forehead for a few seconds. "Body temp's just about eighty degrees. Roughly speaking, I'd say that puts time of death at about ten or twelve hours ago, so … maybe around ten or eleven last night, give or take an hour, maybe two. It's cold in here, so that's a factor. If the door was open all night, that would have accelerated things, so I'll have to check the charts on that. Some blood from the wound on the back of his head and more from his face, but not as much as I'd expect if he'd been alive for long after he sustained this damage."

"I think you're saying that his heart wasn't beating for very long after he took those blows," Saxby said. "Is that what you're thinking?"

"Exactly. Less than a minute is my guess. Preliminary, of course, but seems to fit," Dr. Coyle said. His eyes scanned the surroundings before turning again to the dead man. "Looking at the corner of the counter there, or even just the edge, he could have tripped and fallen against that. Twisted around somehow and hit the back of his head with enough force. And then fell to hit his face square on the floor. That could have done it. I mean, if this was some kind of accident." His gloved hands felt all around the man's face, neck, and skull. "The nose is clearly broken, though there's very little blood or bruising. Feels like at least one break above the eye socket here. The impact on the back of his head feels like a serious crack or dent. I'll have to get a close look at all of this up in my lab."

"If we're thinking maybe it wasn't an accident, and someone else was here and hit him with something heavy," Connor said. "How about that thing on the floor over there. What is that? A candlestick?" He bent down for a close look at an object on the floor a few feet from the body.

"It does look almost like a candlestick, right?" Saxby

said. "Is that what it is? Or some kind of gadget? Looks like a knob or something on the side there. What do you think, Mark?"

"That, my friends, is no candlestick," Dr. Coyle said, moving closer to take a look at the thing. "Are you forgetting your high school science class? Unless I'm very much mistaken, that is a Bunsen burner. The base part of a Bunsen burner. I guess it does look a little like a candlestick, now that you mention it."

"Okay, I remember what that is," Saxby said. "That would make a pretty good blunt instrument to grab if you wanted to whack someone over the head. My memories of that thing are vague at best. Shouldn't it be attached to a gas line, or a propane tank?"

"You're on the right track, Tate," Dr. Coyle said. "But my guess is that it wasn't in operation here. Bunsen burners have been a common lab tool since long before I was born, but they're mostly outdated for modern labs. I'm guessing that, for here, it was a paperweight, or even a decoration. A memento for a science geek, maybe. I don't see any sign of a gas tank or hose."

"The neighbor, Miss Brandt," Brody said, "told us he was a scientist, though she didn't know exactly what kind. She said he worked at that research place in from the beach near the old beach club."

"I know that lab," Dr. Coyle said, "or, I should say I've read about it. They do some kind of research into potential medical applications for marine organisms. I think they're related to the lab over on the bay side that does all the work with horseshoe crabs."

"Got ya, Doc," Saxby said. "I read about the horseshoe

crab thing. Apparently, their blood is critical in vaccine research and testing, if I'm remembering correctly." While he was talking, he had moved farther away between the two long work tables that partly enclosed the rectangular area where the body was laid out. "This does look like a sort of office, or lab, if that's what it is. These counters are desk-height, with the rolling chair so he could zip around from one side to the other. A writing area, books. Any thoughts on what sort of lab this might be, Doc?"

"Hard to say offhand," Dr. Coyle said. He had opened the door of a small mini-fridge that sat under one of the counters. "Small refrigerator, which is totally normal for a science lab, but this one just has nothing but sodas and bottled water. That thing over there is an older model centrifuge. Maybe a hand-me-down from his main place of work. Good quality microscope there, but I don't see any slides out. It doesn't look like an active working lab to me. More like a place to do some occasional homework related to whatever it is he does up there by the beach. Light work, if I can put it that way. No doubt his co-workers could tell you exactly what type of work that is."

"Okay, so, we'll certainly check into all that," Saxby said. "But right now, what do we think happened here? You first, Doctor, please."

Doctor Coyle took a moment to look down at the body and the immediate area. "Well, pending a full autopsy, I'd say likely cause of death was blunt force trauma. If he was here by himself, he could have somehow tripped or stumbled, and fell into the edge or corner of the counter. I guess he could have slipped on those papers on the floor there. But why were they on the floor? Hard to say. If someone else was involved, they could have had an argument that got out of control. The other guy grabbed the Bunsen burner and hit him on the head, causing him to spin around and fall flat on the floor, right on his face. Either that or he hit his head on the counter there, and then down to the floor, where he got the facial injuries. Yeah, blunt force trauma, from one, or two, or even three of those possible impacts."

"That scenario makes a lot of sense to me," Sergeant Vicki Barstow said, having arrived on the scene a few minutes before, joining the group of men around the body. "I mean, either of the possibilities you said, Doctor, but I've got to lean towards the argument or fight idea. If what did the most damage was his head hitting the floor, I like the idea that someone helped him to the floor by hitting him on the back of the head. With that bun burner thing or something else."

"Reasonable thoughts, Sergeant," Dr. Coyle said. "At the moment, I don't see a reason to disagree with any of that."

"There's that little bit of broken glass there, and there," Connor said, pointing first to a spot on the table and then to an area of the floor near the body and almost under the table. "And those papers and pencil look like they could have been shoved aside during a struggle. Coffee mug mostly empty with a little spilled out on the table, like maybe it was jostled. Papers all over, like maybe he was working on something before he was surprised. Also, doesn't that look like some kind of scrape on his right hand? Maybe he fell and tried to catch himself, or tried to break his fall."

"I noticed that too. I'll give it a close look when I get

him on the table," Dr. Coyle said. "You might have it right. A defensive wound is possible too."

"The few things on the floor over there by the other table," Connor continued, "I'm not sure what they are, so not sure if they're supposed to be on the floor or not. More old collectibles maybe, like that Bunsen burner thing. That's about what I see at the moment. What do you think, Chief?"

"I think these are all good observations," Saxby said. "And lots of possibilities to check out. I'm thinking about the one coffee cup. That could imply that he was alone, but it could also just mean that if he had a visitor, he either wasn't a good host, or the visitor didn't want anything. Someone could have popped in to chat and things got heated quickly. In any case, not a lot of clear answers at the moment." He looked at the other officers in turn. "Let's take a very careful look around for anything that tells us he might have had company. Down here and upstairs, okay? We don't know yet if this is a crime scene, but for the moment let's treat it as such. Seems like a good opportunity to use the NikorScan for any prints. Doc, do you need to do anything more with him before we let the guys take him away?"

"No, I don't think so," Dr. Coyle said. "As long as you've got plenty of pictures, I'm done with him until we get him up to my office. After I get a good look at him up there, I'll know more. I'll check out those scrapes on his hand, and anything else I find. I should be able to start on him by late this afternoon." He picked up his bag, and after some brief goodbyes, went out and started down the alley to his car. Saxby motioned to Connor to call in the EMT team.

"I'm going to head out myself," Banks said. "It looks like your team has everything here under control. Got to get back to my full-time job of fighting crime in North Wildwood. Let me know if I can help in any way, or if you just want to bounce ideas around. Good luck with this." He went out after briefly stepping aside to let the EMTs enter with their stretcher.

Saxby went up the stairs to the living area, where he found himself in a small but orderly apartment that consisted mostly of a large open space set up as a fairly traditional living room on one side, with a combined kitchen and dining area on the other. A short stub of a hallway led to a single bedroom across from a large storage closet and a full bathroom. After Sergeant Brody gave him a brief tour of the apartment and updated him on what the other officers had been working on, he called the group together.

"Good work so far, guys. Keep doing what you're doing. I want you to focus on anything that might show that someone else was here last night. Roy, as soon as you can, let's get two officers going through the neighborhood. This may have been an accident, but if not, we need to know if anyone saw or heard anything. You know the drill."

"Already on it, Chief," Brody said. "Hayward and Lathrop got here a few minutes ago and I've got them working the area. I told them just to say that there were reports of a break-in."

"Great. Sounds like you're on top of it, then," Saxby said, nodding. "So, I'll get out of your way. I'm going to grab Vic and head over next door to talk to the neighbor.

Three's downstairs. Coordinate with him on whatever you need. I'll catch up with you both after."

Outside on the brick patio, Saxby and Sergeant Barstow paused for a few minutes to gather their thoughts.

"Well, accident or not, what a damn shame. I hope we can do right by this guy," Saxby said. "While it's all fresh, what's your gut telling you, Vic? First impressions can mean a lot."

After a moment, Barstow said: "There's not enough mess in there to suggest any kind of serious fight. I guess it could have been something fast. Like, just an argument—gets a little passionate, tempers flare up, Person A grabs the nearest weapon and whacks Person B on the head ... I don't know. Hard to say. I'm anxious to hear what the doctor finds."

"Sounds fair," Saxby said, nodding. "We're pretty much on the same page. Hopefully Doctor Coyle will be able to shed some more light. Meanwhile, I think it's time we had a chat with the neighbor who found him—Donna Brandt. Let's see what she can tell us."

Donna Brandt opened the door shortly after Saxby's knock, and showed the two officers upstairs to her eat-in kitchen, where a fresh pot of coffee had just finished brewing.

"That other officer, Connor, I think it was," Brandt said. "He mentioned that you'd likely want to talk to me, so I've been expecting you. Good to meet you both. My God, what a terrible thing. I only knew him—Lewis—to say hello or have a little conversation in passing, but he always seemed like a nice man. Do you know what happened?"

"Not entirely, no. Not just yet," Saxby said. "Until we know more, we can't say if his death was some kind of accident, or if somehow there was foul play involved. I'm sorry that you had to see him like that, but because I know you're an experienced nurse, I'm interested in your impression of what you saw and what you've thought about it. Start from the beginning, if you would please. You went outside to call for your cat? Is that right?"

"Yes, that's right," Brandt said. "I called the police at three after nine. I know that because I checked the time of my call just before you got here. Anyway, so, it must have been about five or six minutes earlier that I opened the door to call for Felix. See, I had let him out at least an hour before, probably right around eight. The thing is, when I let him out around eight, I stepped outside for a minute just for a breath of fresh air—it was such a nice morning. Really, not even a minute, maybe half a minute. But I happened to look over at the other house and saw the door open, like, half-way open."

"And did you see anything else? Or hear anything? Anyone in the area?" Saxby said.

"No, nothing at all, it was very quiet," Brandt said. "Just the birds and a car passing on one of the roads nearby. I didn't think anything of it. Just like, maybe he's about to get something out of his car or something like that. I remember thinking that I probably looked like a wreck, you know, just gotten up and hadn't put my face on yet, that kind of thing. So, I saw the door but that's all, and went back inside. I had some breakfast and did my usual morning routine, and then it must have been no more than a few minutes before nine that I went back outside to call for Felix. The door was still open, just the same amount, and I thought that was odd enough that I walked over to knock. You know, just to let him know he forgot to close his door. He didn't answer so I knocked again, also with no answer. I took one or two steps inside, and that's when I saw his feet sticking out past one of those low work tables."

"Right, that must have been a shock," Saxby said. "And then what? You checked for a pulse?"

Brandt took a moment to take a few breaths followed by a sip of her coffee. "Yes, that's right. I checked for a pulse at his neck, you know, the carotid artery, and didn't get anything. And also, he didn't feel warm at all. More like room temperature. I just knew he must have been dead for hours."

"Did you move the body at all?" Saxby asked. "Or rearrange anything?"

"No, nothing like that," Brandt said. "I mean, aside from that I had to kind of reach around his neck to check for a pulse. He was pretty evenly face down, so I couldn't see the front of him. I mean, I could see just enough to know it was him, but that's all. It was a shock, you know, but I remember looking around and thinking at the moment that he must have fallen and hit his head somehow. It occurred to me that he might have had a stroke or a heart attack. A seizure even, but of course I don't know anything at all about his health. That's about it. I came back over here for my phone, and called the police right away. I waited outside after that, and your Deputy Connor was here within a few minutes."

"Now, you've already told us that you only knew him in passing," Saxby said, "but is there anything at all you can tell us about any family, or regular friends you might have seen coming or going?"

"Well, no, I can't really think of anything," Brandt said. "I mean, it was somewhat common to see a car in the alley, like, sometimes a flash of headlights or something like that, but I can't say that meant he was having company. Sometimes people park back here and then go to one of the houses on the main road. I don't think I ever spoke with him long enough to hear about any family. Sorry, I guess I'm not a very observant neighbor."

"Oh no, that's all fine. Just questions we need to ask," Saxby said. "Well, again, I realize that you've been through a shock, and it certainly seems like you handled it all very well. We appreciate you sharing all this with us so clearly. Sergeant?" He looked over to Barstow with a slight nod, throwing the interview her way.

"I have to agree with the chief that we appreciate your help with this," Barstow said. "How about last night? Can you tell us about that? Were you home, did you hear or see anything? Anything at all could help."

"Sure. Yesterday was Sunday, so I had a fairly lazy day," Brandt said. "I did my grocery shopping early, at the Acme, then a few other errands. I'd say I was home for the day by about three or so. Like most Sundays, a friend of mine came over for dinner, and after that we watched some TV. 'Netflix and chill' is what I think some people call it. You know, just hang out with some wine and a good show."

"That sounds nice," Barstow said. "I've heard that term too. Do you remember what time your friend left?"

"Well, on that, I do remember," Brandt said, "within maybe ten minutes, because we watched an episode more than we had planned, and it was late. We were in suspense to see what happens next, you see? I think Mallory left at right about ten-thirty, give or take a few."

"Mallory? That wouldn't be Mallory Vickers, would it?" Barstow said.

"Why yes, that's my friend's name," Brandt said. "Mallory Vickers. She only lives about five or six blocks away, but she drove over. If you remember, it was windy last night, and it was a chilly wind. Do you know Mallory?"

"I wouldn't say I know her," Barstow said. "But we've met and spoken a few times. She was helpful to the police with a case we had about a year ago. Nice young lady as I recall. So, you think she left at about half past ten? Did you walk out with her at that time?"

"No, we were both pretty tired. I started to finish with cleaning up the dinner things, and she went downstairs and let herself out. Her car was about halfway up the alley. You know, maybe you should ask her if she heard or saw anything as she was leaving."

Saxby and Barstow left shortly after Brandt gave them the contact information for Mallory Vickers. Out on the small patio, they paused for a moment.

"I can't help but feel sorry for these two ladies," Barstow said. "Mallory Vickers was the one who found Boone Roseman's body last year, and this morning, her friend over here gets to find her neighbor's body. What a bizarre thing to have in common."

"You're right about that, Vic," Saxby said. "Bizarre and also sad. Well, look, I'm going to go back in and check on how things are coming along with the crime scene work. After that, I'm going to make a pit-stop at the station, then I'll head over to the lab where he worked and see what there is to see over there. Far as I can guess, they wouldn't even know yet that anything's happened to the guy."

"I guess you're right, Chief," Barstow said. "Unless he had a day off scheduled, they're probably wondering why he's late for work about now. They'll be hearing about him from you."

"Yeah, Vic, it looks that way," Saxby said. "All in a day's work. Listen, in the meantime, I'd like you to go ahead and see if you can find this Mallory Vickers and see what she has to say about last night. Maybe she saw or heard something that Brandt didn't. If this is a crime, you'll be lead on the case and we'll work together on it. Let's catch up at the station by late afternoon."

"I'm on it, Chief," Barstow said. "Looks like the week is off to a hell of a start."

3

Thirty minutes later, Saxby drove through the small and exclusive neighborhood of custom beach houses that made up one of the quietest corners of Cape May in the far-eastern part of town. A long, wide beach was over the dunes to the right, and a large tract of preserved marshland was beyond the houses off to the left. A hundred yards past the last house was the private beach club, closed for the season, that he had been to only once when attending the wedding reception of a wealthy friend years ago. After that, at the end of the narrow lane came a low rectangular building on the edge of a sand-swept parking lot that looked about half-full.

The building was a bland, businesslike cinderblock and cement box, sturdily built, and painted in a neutral shade of yellowish-beige that helped it to fit in well with its placement at the base of the dunes. A long line of block lettering ran along the upper edge of the building, proclaiming the place to be the "Cape Shore Marine Research Center."

Saxby counted six other cars in the lot as he walked to the glass door at the center of the building's façade. The door was firmly locked, and looking through it into what appeared to be a small waiting area, he didn't see anyone. To the right of the door was a doorbell, with a small speaker mounted above that, and a fish-eyed surveillance camera another foot above that. He pressed the button on the doorbell, and after a few seconds a disembodied voice came out of the speaker.

"Yes, hello, Officer. I'll be right there to open the door."

The door was opened a moment later by a bespectacled and smiling fiftyish man in a white lab coat.

"Good morning, Officer," the man said. "Please come inside. How can we help?"

"Good morning," Saxby said. "Chief Tate Saxby of the Cape May City Police Department. And you are?"

"I'm sorry, Chief Saxby," the man said. "I'm Doctor James Olson. I'm the manager here at the lab. As you can see, we don't have a receptionist. We don't have many visitors, and rarely anyone as important as the chief of police. What can I do for you?"

"Nice to meet you, Dr. Olson," Saxby said. "I'm here about a man by the name of Lewis Forbes. Am I correct in thinking that he works here with you?"

"Why, yes, Lewis is one of us," Olson said. "But I'm afraid he's not here right now, though I can't say why. I've tried to call him several times and left messages."

"Well, Dr. Olson, I'm sorry to say that Dr. Forbes won't be hearing those messages," Saxby said. "Is there somewhere private we can talk? Your office?" He saw the look of confusion on Dr. Olson's face move quickly to shock, and then just as quickly to something that Saxby decided was a sort of sad resignation, all in a span of about fifteen seconds.

A matter-of-fact person, Saxby thought to himself, with a slight feeling of relief.

"I see. Or, I think I see, that is," Olson said. "Um, yes, why don't we continue this in my office."

Olson led the way down a long hallway that ran parallel to the front of the building, first passing a wide set of windows that looked into a large and brightly lit laboratory. Several counter-height workstations were occupied by white-clad people engrossed in their work. Saxby judged that the open-plan lab must have taken up about half of the building. After the lab came a series of four doors that he thought must be individual offices for some of the resident scientists, by virtue of the plastic nametag mounted to each door. Olson showed him into the last office in the row, which appeared to be larger than the others.

"So, is he—Lewis I mean—are you saying something happened to him? Is he dead?" Olson said, after both men had taken a seat at a small round table that shared the office with a large desk in a mass-produced institutional style, along with several chairs.

"Yes, I'm afraid so, Doctor," Saxby said. "A neighbor found him in his apartment early this morning. It looks like it may have been some sort of freak accident that killed him, though I will tell you in confidence that we are looking into the possibility that there could have been foul play involved."

Olson's face again took on an expression of shock.

Saxby raised a hand to cut him off before he could speak. "Let me add, Doctor, that when police find a body, depending on the immediate surroundings and circumstances, it is completely routine to go through the basic steps to rule out foul play. Many times it's very obvious, other times it's less so. So please keep that under your hat for now. I understand you're going to want to inform your staff about this right away, and I'm asking you to please frame it as just an accidental death. And simply, that's all you know. Can I count on you for that?"

"Yes, sure. I can do that, Chief Saxby," Olson said. "And I do understand your point about the need to do some investigation as a matter of routine. I am a scientist, as are the rest of us here, so the need to get to the facts is a way of life for us. With that said, can you tell me anything at all about what happened?"

"Sure, I'll tell you what I can," Saxby said, "which, frankly, isn't much at the moment. Dr. Forbes' apartment is two floors, with the living area on the upper level, and the lower level mostly set up as a combination of workspace and storage area. He had a small office, and what I'll call a lab set up in that area, though nothing like the serious lab you have here, with all the bright lights and modern equipment. I gather he took work home on occasion. That's where he was found, early this morning. It appears he may have fallen and hit his head hard enough for it to be fatal. That's how it looks on the face of it. Though, as I've already mentioned, we have to consider all possibilities. It looks like this probably happened late yesterday evening."

"Oh my God, how terrible," Olson said. "I just, well, it's

taking me a minute to process that this really happened, so please bear with me. I can only hope he didn't suffer."

"The medical examiner has a lot of work to do yet," Saxby said, "but with what we know so far, it looks like he probably passed very quickly. We hope to have more details on that soon. Would you know anything about any family? Either around here or otherwise? Anyone we can contact?"

"I really don't, no," Olson said. "I have the feeling he was alone in the area, but I can't recall him ever actually telling me that. Maybe it's just something I heard. Some of the other people he worked with here might be of more help to you on that."

"Sure, and that makes sense," Saxby said. "I may want to talk with them at some point, but for now, let's keep this with just the two of us. Doctor, can you give me a summary of what this place is, what kind of work you do here, what kind of work Dr. Forbes would have been doing – that sort of thing. A general picture, please."

"Of course, Chief Saxby," Olson said, "that would be my pleasure, though I think that calls for a cup of coffee. May I interest you?" He started working with a K-cup machine on the credenza near his desk, with Saxby accepting the offer with a nod. They fixed their coffees as Olson started his summary, continuing as they returned to their seats.

"There are eight of us here—well, seven now, sorry. Not used to that just yet. So yes, aside from myself, there are six other scientists working here. Our focus, in a general sense, is on a number of potential applications of marine animal proteins in human medicine. Specifically, marine mollusks. To put it another way, we and other facilities like us, look for ways that the tissue or secretions from bottom-dwelling marine mollusks, such as clams or scallops, might be useful in developing treatments for human illness."

"And the shallow waters along the New Jersey coast are loaded with those kinds of animals," Saxby said. "Though I imagine not to the extent that they were, say, a hundred years ago."

"That's correct," Olson continued. "The vast and relatively shallow and sandy underwater terrain off the New Jersey coast is rich in bottom-dwelling sea life. As you point out, not as rich as it once was, but still an active population and robust breeding ground. Our research here, for the last year or so, has been concerned with scallops to a great extent. As someone who's obviously familiar with the area, you must know that this is very much 'scallop country'."

"Yes. I did know that," Saxby said. "I don't know a lot about scallops, but I did know that. Scallop boats have been a major part of South Jersey fishing fleets for as far back as I can remember. Is that what Dr. Forbes was working on?"

"Yes, along with several other team members," Olson said. "For most of the last year or so, his efforts have been focused on certain enzymes found in Atlantic scallops that appear to hold substantial promise for the treatment of Alzheimer's disease. Nothing is set in stone just yet, but the possibilities are very exciting."

"And as far as you know," Saxby said, "was he seen as a good team member? Did he get along well with the others?"

"Oh yes, I think so," Olson said. "I'm not aware of any substantial friction in our lab. There would be disagreements now and then, of course. Part of doing the work of science is being able to disagree freely. You disagree, then you discuss, do more research, and discuss again. That's all natural and desirable. But yes, as far as I know, Lewis was well respected and worked well with the others. This has been a fairly tranquil workplace overall."

"Now, bearing in mind what we discussed earlier," Saxby said, "about the routine need to look at all possibilities, was your relationship with Dr. Forbes such that you knew much about his personal life? For example, any problems he was having with people outside of work? Romantic breakups, anything like that?"

"Hmmm, no, I had a friendly relationship with Lewis," Olson said, "but I wouldn't say that we were friends. He was single, as far as I know, unless he really kept that part of his life secret. I heard him mention once or twice something about meeting this friend or that, or watching the game with a friend, that kind of thing. You know, now that you ask, I realize I knew almost nothing about his life outside of here. I must imagine that some of the other people here would know more about him in that respect than I do, since they've worked together more closely. My own research has been more of a solo variety." Olson opened one of the file drawers in his desk and, after a brief search, pulled out a few stapled sheets. He passed them over the desk to Saxby. "Here's a list of all the people who work here, including myself, in case you need it. That's current and has everyone's contact information. You can have that copy."

"Thank you, Doctor," Saxby said, folding the document into thirds. "If this turns out to be something other than a tragic accident, I'm sure we'll want to talk to everyone. But for now, I think I've taken enough of your time and I'll let you get back to work. I know you'll be wanting to meet with your people about Dr. Forbes. Please, Doctor, as we discussed, we're only just starting to investigate, and what happened to Dr. Forbes is just an accident as far as we can tell."

"Understood, Chief Saxby," Olson said. "That's how I'll frame it for the time being, and I hope you will let me know how else we can help."

Back in the foyer, just as he was reaching for the door, a thought that had been simmering deep in Saxby's mind suddenly bubbled up to become a lucid idea, and he turned back to Dr. Olson.

"Just something I thought of as I was driving in here, past all these million-dollar homes, and the private beach club. I can't imagine what the costs are to buy land and build right here. It seems like a strange place to locate an office or a research lab. Doesn't that seem odd to you?"

Olson smiled and let out a brief chuckle. "It does seem a little odd on the surface, doesn't it? But then you haven't seen the beach side of the building. We have a small pier that allows us to dock our two research boats. Nothing fancy, just a pair of Boston Whalers, twenty-four footers, equipped differently. They're in the harbor right now, but when there's a need for them, we have a local man who maintains them and drives them for us. This place was built before my time, but no doubt the need for the boats is part of the reason for our location. I agree with you that this must be an expensive spot, but our corporate backers, the Fisheries Council, has deep pockets. Which is essential, because we don't currently get any help from the government. Would you like to see the pier?"

"Oh, no need for that right now, Doctor," Saxby said, pushing open the door to the parking lot, "but thank you. Maybe next time. Anyway, thank you for your help, and please accept my condolences for your team's loss. Please contact me if anything else comes to mind relative to what we talked about, and otherwise, I'll be in touch."

4

It was early afternoon, four hours after the body of Lewis Forbes had been found, when Sergeant Barstow appeared in the doorway of Saxby's office in the Cape May police station. As Saxby looked up from the stack of paperwork he'd been working on, Deputy Connor popped up next to Barstow.

"Got a sec, Chief?" Barstow said.

"Sure, Vic, Three," Saxby said. "Is it time for us to talk?"

"We think so, Chief," Connor said. "Lots to talk about in fact. We were thinking about grabbing some takeout and going over everything in the conference room. You able to interrupt for that?"

Saxby looked at his watch before spreading his arms in a stretch. "You know what, yes. That all sounds good. Just tell me first, though—how's it looking? Accident or no accident?"

"Not conclusive yet, Chief," Connor said, "but it's looking like someone else was there. I'm thinking a fight or a scuffle that went south somehow."

"Agreed from my end," Barstow said, "though we still need to hear from Dr. Coyle."

Reminding himself to try to maintain decorum in front of his junior officers, Saxby kept his "oh shit" exclamation at a low volume, though not low enough to fool Barstow or Connor. "Okay, well, if that's what it is, then it is what it is, and we'll do what we do. I look forward to hearing what you've found. Where were you thinking for food?"

"Just down to Starla's," Barstow said. "She's been having some really good lunch specials lately."

"That's what I was hoping you'd say," Saxby said. "Ask her to give me my regular, but with chips instead of fries. Get whatever you're getting and put it all on my account."

"Chief, you don't have to do that every time we offer to pick up lunch," Barstow said.

"I know that," Saxby said. "But if we're going to work through lunch together, I figure the least I can do is buy you a sandwich. Okay? That's an order. Give me a yell when you get back."

As they were unwrapping their sandwiches at the conference room table, Saxby was the first to bring up the business at hand. The conversation went from there as the three of them ate lunch. "Can I assume you've heard from Brody as far as anything they might have found around the neighborhood?"

"Yes, we have," Barstow said. "He filled us in as soon as they got back, but it's not much. They knocked on about twenty doors and only found half of the places to be occupied. As you know, a lot of houses are closed up for the season at this point. For most of the people they found, nobody was aware of anything unusual in the area late last night, except for one person who thought he might have heard someone yelling. I'll tell you more about that after I tell you about Mallory Vickers."

"So, you were able to get her, that's great," Saxby said. "Monday morning. I'm surprised she wasn't at work."

"Lucky break for us on that," Barstow said. "She's covering the second shift for a co-worker this week. She remembered me from that last thing, you know, when she found Boone Roseman. She was very glad to try to help. What she told me about last night lines up just fine with what the neighbor, Donna Brandt, told us. She remembered leaving at about ten-thirty. That's where there might be something interesting. She was parked near the end of the alley, so only had about a one-minute walk to her car, but she thought she heard people yelling. She said she stopped and looked around for a minute. Didn't hear anything clearly, just more like something off in the near distance, like a block or half a block away. When I asked her if it could have been coming from Forbes' apartment, she said that had occurred to her but she decided it wasn't. She did say that she saw the lights on, and she was pretty sure the door was closed."

"It sounds like she's saying she stopped and looked around," Saxby said, "but didn't end up identifying where the yelling—if that's what it was—was coming from. Do I have that right?"

"Yes, pretty much," Barstow said. "She mostly figured whatever she heard must have been from one of the houses across the back lawns on Washington Street, but couldn't really say."

"But then, the thing with that," Connor said, "is that after Vic met with her, we went over there and did a little bit of testing. Unscientific, but interesting. Megan helped us out before the end of her shift. She and I moved around the area a little bit, inside the apartment, in the alley, and then on both of the main roads. And we yelled."

"And I hope you managed to do this without terrifying the local residents, right?" Saxby said.

"You bet, Chief," Connor said. "Like I said, most of the houses in the area are empty anyway."

"So, Three and Officer Hayward—Megan I mean," Barstow said, "did some talking and yelling from a few different spots while I stood in the alley about where Mallory Vickers would have been walking to her car, and listened. Like Three said, our findings aren't very scientific, but it seemed to us that if someone was yelling, or people were arguing inside the apartment, it could easily sound to someone in the alley that it was actually coming from farther away, like on either main road. I'm guessing it has to do with the acoustics of the alley, like a tunnel effect maybe, with all the overhanging trees and the back walls of the sheds.

"And then there's the guy I mentioned before, who thought he might have heard people arguing when he took out the trash about ten-thirty. He was in the area that Mallory Vickers thought the sound might have been coming from, but he told Lathrop that he didn't hear anything near him. He wasn't sure either, but he thought it was probably coming from over where Mallory Vickers was in the alley."

"Interesting. It was windy last night, which could certainly skew the perception of where distant voices were coming from," Saxby said. "So, we've got two witnesses who think they may have heard raised voices in the area, and they each think it was coming from around where the other person was. How does that stand up against the testing you did?"

Connor looked briefly at Barstow, who gave him a nod. "Well, again, it's nothing conclusive, but based on what these two people told us, along with our testing, and the wind, there could have been a loud argument going on inside Forbes' apartment and it could easily have sounded like it was coming from farther away. For example, if Mallory Vickers was in the middle of the alley and thought she heard yelling way down the block, then yes, we think it could have been coming from inside the apartment just forty or fifty feet from her."

"That's not much to go on, Chief," Barstow said, "but it sounds like there was a heated exchange going on in the area right at that time, and it could very well have been inside the apartment."

"Okay, got it," Saxby said. "Good work on that, then. That's something to start with. What else did you find that makes you think Forbes had company?"

"Well, you saw where he was laying out on the floor," Connor said. "With the papers scattered all around, pens, the coffee cup—all pretty messy, like whatever was on the counter had been knocked or shoved off. One of the sheets of paper on the floor had a partial footprint on it from some shoe other than what Forbes was wearing. He was wearing a pair of fairly new L.L. Bean slippers, but the footprint was from something more like a man's dress shoe."

Saxby said: "And you're confident that print couldn't be from one of us there at the scene?"

"Pretty much, Chief, pending results from the lab," Connor said. "One of the first pictures the guys got shortly after finding him appears to show the sheet of paper in question about two or three feet from the body. It's hard to see but I think you can make out the shoe print if you look really close. Anyway, we got pictures of the shoes of everyone who was there and sent them up with the paper. I also sent up a little bit of the brick dust from the patio outside. I thought the print had a reddish tint to it, so I'm thinking some visitor picked up a little of that dust walking up to Forbes' door, and then stepped on the paper some-time later."

"What about any cameras in the area?" Saxby said. "No banks or other businesses, but these days a lot of private homes have cameras on them for one reason or other. Any luck on that?"

"Doesn't look like it, Chief," Connor said. "We did find two houses with those new doorbell cameras, but both of those houses appear to be empty. I've already asked Doreen to track down the owners to see if anything was active and might have picked something up, but I figure that's a long shot."

"Agreed, but a long shot that's still worth checking out," Saxby said. "Anything else?"

"As far as showing that someone else was there with

Forbes," Barstow said, "no, not really, other than the obvious circumstantial. Without jumping the gun on Dr. Coyle, it sure did look to me like someone must have whacked him on the head. Then we have the open door. He was there in his own place, working on whatever, in his slippers. There wasn't any reason for the door to be open, unless someone else left it open as they left. As they were running out maybe. That's about what we have. Did you get out to his work place earlier?"

"Yes, I did," Saxby said. "Out there just past the old beach club. First time I was ever there. I met with the person in charge, a Dr. James Olson, who filled me in on what the place was and some of what they work on out there. Sounds like their current focus is on scallops, and trying to find ways they can be useful in treatments for diseases. He mentioned Alzheimer's disease in particular, which Forbes was working on. He didn't seem to have known Forbes very well personally, but thought he had been well liked and respected. Apart from Olson, with Forbes gone, there are now six other scientists working there. I didn't speak with any of them, but I did get a list of all their contact information. If this turns into a case of murder or manslaughter, we'll need to get right on meeting with those people. If somebody did kill him, or fight with him, somebody he worked with every day is a good possibility."

"Did this Dr. Olson know anything about Forbes' family?" Barstow asked. "Maybe someone in the area we could talk to? Maybe he was married at some time in the past."

"I did ask him about that," Saxby said, "and he told me he just didn't know the man that well on a personal level.

He did say that he thought Forbes had good relationships with his co-workers, so I'm hoping we can learn more about him from those people if we need to."

"Hmmm. And the neighbor lady we met with earlier," Barstow said, "didn't know anything either. I know it's only been hours since we found him, but I can't help but get the feeling that the guy was a real loner."

"I'm with you on that," Saxby said, "but let's give it some time and see how it plays out. The warrant for his place should be ready by tomorrow, then we'll be able to look at his appointment book or address book if he has any, and we can start to flesh out some details. When we're done here, I'll pop out to the front desk and ask Doreen to see what she can dig up on Forbes too. We'll get there. If that's all, I've got a quick meeting with the mayor, then I'll be back in my office. Don't hesitate to interrupt me."

With both Barstow and Connor indicating they had nothing further to add, and the last of the lunch debris gathered up, the meeting broke up and the three of them went their separate ways. Saxby went out to the outer office to speak with Officer Doreen Watson at the dispatch desk. A fully certified officer for more than thirty years, Doreen served primarily as the main dispatcher and office manager for the police station, as well as being a sort of "mother hen" for Saxby and the other officers. With her having seen a number of police chiefs and mayors come and go over the years, Saxby knew her as one of the most valuable constants in his life.

"Good afternoon, Doreen. Anything exciting going on out here today?"

"Nothing much at the moment, Chief," Doreen said.

"And with this being the police station, I'm pretty sure that's a good thing. A quiet day is a good thing, but then you had quite a morning, didn't you. Do you know yet if the late Dr. Forbes met with some kind of foul play?"

"Not entirely sure yet," Saxby said, "but there are some indications that there was probably someone there with him last night, which may well point in that direction. I'm waiting to hear from Dr. Coyle."

"I see. I'll watch for a call from him and put it through right away," Doreen said. "Three asked me to look into a few things for him, and I'll have something on that soon. Is there anything else I can do to help?"

"Yes, there is, actually," Saxby said. "I'd like you to do some general research on Dr. Lewis Forbes. Anything biographical you can find. Is there a marriage license out there somewhere, divorce maybe, siblings, children—anything at all. I'll probably be talking with his co-workers, which should give us some details, but aside from that, we hardly know anything about the man at the moment. Whatever you can find could help."

"Yes sireee, Chief," Doreen said. "I'll start on that and get back to you as soon as I can."

They chatted for a few more minutes before Saxby started back to his office, thinking about the pile of paperwork that needed his attention, and potentially meeting with Mayor Jack Torrance. He wondered to himself if he would soon need to be telling the mayor about their fourth murder case in as many years. *No—let's not jump the gun. Forbes probably just fell and hit his head.*

The logical part of Saxby tried to find a way to like that idea, but his gut was having trouble buying it.

5

It was just past seven-thirty when Saxby finished tidying up his kitchen after dinner. Having enjoyed a large glass of red wine with his re-heated penne bolognese, he was looking forward to pouring another and relaxing in his den for a while. He was in the process of deciding between reading a book or looking for a movie to watch when his cell phone rang. He scooped it up from the counter, noting that the call was coming from Dr. Coyle.

"Hey, Mark," Saxby answered. "I wasn't expecting to hear from you so soon."

"Well, as it happens," Dr. Coyle said, "I needed to come back into town to pick up some stuff from my aunt's house, so here I am. I was able to work on the late Dr. Forbes this afternoon, and I have some information for you. I don't have the full report ready yet, but I can give you a preliminary if you like. Are you busy?"

"No, I'm all yours," Saxby said. "Why don't you come on over?"

Saxby gave him the address, and Dr. Coyle was there

within ten minutes. They settled onto stools along one side of the expansive kitchen island, and Saxby poured out two glasses of a favorite Napa cabernet, explaining that his fiancée, Angela, was covering a late shift and wouldn't be home for several hours.

"Ah, I figured that was probably it," Dr. Coyle said. "Tell her I said hello and we'll hope for next time. Well, look, Tate, I am going to enjoy your excellent wine and hang out for a little while, but I won't keep you for long. You've been very patient, but I'm sure you're anxious to hear what I've found so far."

"Sounds good, Mark," Saxby said. "So yeah, spill the beans and we'll have that out of the way. Was it an accident or something else?"

"I wish I could say it was just an accident, but no, it really isn't looking that way. Cause of death, as we suspected, was blunt force trauma to the head and neck, coming from two different blows, or impacts. Do you remember that old Bunsen burner that was lying on the floor not too far from the body? The contours of the base match the indentation in the rear side of his skull—about here." The doctor used his hand to indicate an area high on his head about midway between the left ear and the back of the skull. "It's pretty clear to me that someone picked it up and whacked Forbes on the head very hard. Hard enough to crack the skull. When I took a close look under magnification, I could make out something like a hashmark on the bone that matched the knurled knob on the side of the burner. Now, whether Person X grabbed the thing and swung it during an argument, or maybe did something stealthier—like sneaking up behind Forbes somehow—I can't say with any certainty."

"Okay, I get that," Saxby said. "And you said there was a second impact, right? The first whack on the head didn't kill him?"

"I think the first hit probably would have killed him, given a half-hour or so and lacking very prompt medical attention, but I'd say it was the next impact, seconds later probably, that really did the job. Without stepping on your police-toes too much, my theory of what likely happened is that Forbes was stunned by the blow on the head with the burner base, and immediately fell down, hitting the edge or corner of the counter with enough force to crack at least two of the uppermost cervical vertebrae. The impact point was rear-center, just about where the neck meets the base of the skull. I figure he may have spun around from the first blow, in order to then hit the counter the way he did."

"So, you're saying both of those blows were on or near the rear of his head," Saxby said. "But there was also some injury to his face, wasn't there?"

"There was some substantial injury to his face, yes, but nothing that would have caused death," Dr. Coyle said. "Some scrapes, a cracked cheekbone, and his nose was broken, all as a result of his final contact with the cement floor, but the deadly stuff came before that. It's likely that he was knocked unconscious by the first blow with the Bunsen burner, but if not, certainly with the second—the counter. In any case, he was out cold within seconds, and dead within a very short time. Two or three minutes maybe, and that's on the high side."

"Sounds like the poor guy really bounced around in the worst possible way," Saxby said. "Anything you can tell me about the assailant?"

"A little, maybe," Dr. Coyle said. "But it'll sound like millions of people. Certainly, someone as tall as Forbes or a few inches taller. Let's just say between about five-ten and six-two. Forbes was five-ten. And obviously whoever it was had to be very strong, in order to swing that burner with so much force. So, a strong man within a few inches of six feet is my guess. Could have been a woman with the same qualities, but as you know, that's statistically unlikely. Sorry, Tate. I told you it wasn't much. That's about it for now. I'll get you the report tomorrow. Could be later afternoon."

"Great. I'll watch for that, but I appreciate that you got back to me with this much as quickly as you did. You know how time is of the essence with these things, and this helps get the wheels turning. Dammit. Here we go again with this. It's gonna be a busy day tomorrow." Saxby picked up the wine bottle and tilted it against the light, before pouring the rest into their glasses. "Here, there's not much left. Maybe we can enjoy a second glass with a more pleasant topic of conversation."

Dr. Coyle took his wine glass with him as he stood up and walked the perimeter of the kitchen, stopping to admire the array of pots hanging from a rack. "This is the first time I've been in your new house. How long have you been here? About a year?"

"Yeah, I guess that's right. About a year," Saxby said. "Took me a while to get used to it, but I like it, and Angela's happy with it. We each have our own office, and she's got a giant walk-in closet with room for all her shoes and handbags."

"And you inherited your cousin's whole business empire, right?" Dr. Coyle said. "The Harbor House, the construction business, a hotel or two. That must be a lot to juggle, along with being the chief of police. How do you handle it all?"

Saxby laughed and took a sip of wine. "Well, mostly, the way I handle it is that I don't handle it. I mean, I'm lucky to have a bunch of good people in place who I trust to run things, with Angela being number one. She's actually the general manager of the restaurant division. I'm not totally hands-off, but I prefer to let the people who know what they're doing more than I do handle the day-to-day stuff so I can focus on my police work. Probably in the future I'll have to move more towards the company, but there's no need for that yet."

"Well, that's good, because I'm not in any hurry to have to break in a new police chief," Dr. Coyle said. He drained the last of his wine and set the empty glass on the counter. "It's getting late. I'd better get back over to the house. Thanks for the wine. I'll get back on the case tomorrow and get you the full report on Forbes. Give my best to Angela."

After Saxby saw his friend out, he fixed himself a cup of coffee and took it into his office at the rear of the house. The first thing he did was put in a call to Sergeant Barstow, giving her a compact version of what he'd learned from the doctor.

"Well, Vic, it is what it is. I had hoped the doc would tell us it was an accident, but it looks like we've got another murder on our hands. Or manslaughter at least. Let's plan to hit the ground running tomorrow."

6

"Somebody killed Lewis Forbes late Sunday night," Saxby said, as he paced along one side of the conference room table with coffee mug in hand. "Though, based on what we know so far from Dr. Coyle, his assailant may not have intended it to go that far."

"Ah … I don't know, Chief," Barstow said, "that was a hell of a whack on his head with that Bunsen thing."

"Absolutely, I understand that," Saxby said. "I'm not suggesting anyone gets a pass for hitting a person on the head. I'm just keeping in mind that it could have been a situation where there was an argument that might have ended with Person X leaving Forbes' place in a huff, but instead escalated and got out of hand. The combination of anger and adrenaline can do that kind of thing. Working with what little we know at the moment, I consider it a possibility that Person X became enraged enough to hit Forbes on the head with the nearest heavy object, and then was surprised and maybe freaked out when the guy fell against the counter and was killed."

"Okay, I get your point," Barstow said. "It could have been like a moment of passion that turned into 'Oh my God, what have I done' kinda thing. Of course we need to keep that in mind."

"Right. That's all I'm saying," Saxby said. "Everything's on the table right now. One thing about my scenario is: that would probably rule out premeditated murder. Some kind of crime of passion would become more likely. Which brings me to my next question, and that is: What are the main reasons people kill each other? Let's take premeditated murder first. We can't rule that out yet. Three?"

"Well, hmmm. I think the reasons for premeditated murder might be easier to list than for a crime of passion," Connor said. "Why do people plan and prepare to kill? Money, drugs, and love are the biggies. The problem we have with Forbes right now is that we really don't know anything about the guy yet, other than that he was a scientist working on ways to cure disease. It's not like he worked in a top-secret weapons factory or something like that. Nobody would have killed him for his work."

"You're right that we don't know enough about him yet," Saxby said. "I can't imagine it was any kind of love-triangle type situation, but we need to know more about his personal life before we can rule it out entirely. Same for drugs. Seems very unlikely, but again, we can't rule it out just yet."

At that moment, Doreen popped her head into the conference room. "Sorry to interrupt, folks, but I wanted to let you know the search warrant came through just now from county. Judge Zimmerman signed it first thing this morning. How are you doing on coffee?"

"That's great news. Thank you, Doreen," Saxby said. "I think we're good on the coffee for now. Meeting's almost over."

"The warrant should be a big help," Barstow said. "We'll know a lot more about him after a close look around his place."

"Let's hope so," Saxby said. "That, and talking to anyone who knew him. So, when Brody and his crew talked to whoever they could find in the neighborhood, they didn't find anybody who knew a thing about Forbes—do I have that right?"

"That's right, Chief," Connor said. "Apart from maybe a wave at the neighbor taking out the trash or walking the dog or whatever, nobody seemed to know him."

"And it's the same story with the neighbor who found him," Barstow said. "Donna Brandt. She hardly knew anything about him either."

"That's right. Just the quiet neighbor who kept to himself," Saxby said. "Okay. So, aside from that, as far as any human contact, all we have is the other people who worked at the lab. Meeting with those people and executing the search warrant are our top priorities. Three, I'd like you to work with Brody on getting the search started right away. I already talked with him about it yesterday and he's expecting to handle that. He should be able to grab at least two of the other officers. Got it?"

"I got it, Chief," Connor said. "I'll get with him right away and we'll start that moving along."

"Great, thanks," Saxby said. "And don't be surprised if you see me over there later. I'll pop in if I get time." Conner nodded at that and left the room, leaving Saxby with Sergeant Barstow.

"That leaves you and I to handle the scientists," Saxby said. "There are six of them along with the head man, Dr. Olson. I'll give him a heads-up that we'll be coming over to speak to his people. I'm sure he'll be able to loan us a room for a little while. I'm thinking let's meet with them together, maybe ten or fifteen minutes for each person, and see how it goes. Do they know anything about Forbes' personal life, anyone who might want to do him harm, any family they're aware of—you know the drill."

"Sure, Chief," Barstow said. "And their own relationship with Forbes. How closely did they work together, how did they get along, like that. We don't have any suspects yet, but these people aren't excluded, far as I know."

"No, you're absolutely right," Saxby said. "There's nothing at the moment that says our assailant couldn't be someone he worked with. Respectful to everyone, no suspects at the moment, just filling in background and trying to learn what we can about Lewis Forbes."

After Saxby and Barstow finished with their interviews of the scientists at the marine research center two hours later, they lingered in Barstow's cruiser in the parking lot for a few minutes, discussing their impressions.

"Well, that was an interesting bunch," Barstow said. "Smart as can be, but not really people people."

"That's putting it diplomatically," Saxby said with a quick

laugh. "But I will say that they seemed to be genuinely sorry about Forbes, even if he wasn't close with any of them. As Dr. Olson mentioned to me when I was here yesterday, 'friendly, but not friends.' So, the guy Forbes worked most closely with was Dr. Hill. Arthur Hill. Buttoned up pretty tight, but I got the impression that he was very affected."

"That's the main impression I got from him too," Barstow said. "But I have to say, I also thought he was a little evasive. I mean, not that he refused to answer anything, just more like a feeling that he was on guard. I'm not sure how. Just something off. Did you get that too?"

"You know, I did, a bit. A lot like you describe, but I was waiting to see if you brought it up first," Saxby said. "Let's remember that people react to terrible news differently, but don't dismiss your feelings. I've seen them be right before. Let's just make a note of it for now."

"Right, got it," Barstow said. "Anyway, at least now we know a little more about the work they do at the lab, and that there's an ex-wife and a niece out there somewhere we need to find. I'll start working on tracking them down."

Saxby's cell phone rang and he tapped the screen to take the call, seeing it was from Deputy Connor. "What's up, Three? Are you still over at Forbes' apartment?"

"Yeah, Chief, we're all still here but wrapping up soon," Connor said. "We've been finding some good info here. A couple of things to follow up on. You think you'd be able to stop by?"

"Vic and I just finished up here a few minutes ago," Saxby said. "We'll be there in five."

~

Returning to Lewis Forbes' apartment after parking near the end of the alley, Saxby and Barstow were greeted just inside the door by Sergeant Brody. "We're just wrapping up here, Chief. Three's got a list of a few things we thought you should know about. Couple things to follow up on that might be of some help. You'll find him upstairs in the kitchen."

"Okay, thanks, Roy. I can't wait to see what you've all found. Good work by all of you."

Saxby and Barstow went up the stairs, where they found Connor sitting at the small kitchen table making notes on a legal pad. Officers Redding and Stockton greeted them briefly on their way out.

"Hey, Chief, Vic, glad you could make it over," Connor said. "How did the interviews with the scientists go?"

"Oh, I think they went well," Saxby said. "No great revelations. It looks like Dr. Forbes was something of a cypher. He put a lot into his work and a lot less into his social life, is how it looks."

"But we did learn that he was married at some point years ago," Barstow said, "and that he occasionally talked about a niece he was very fond of, though nobody knew her name or anything about her parents. Having a niece would seem to indicate that you also have at least one brother or sister, so there's that."

"Well, I can add something to the niece story," Connor said. He gestured to a pile of papers and other small items on the table. "But I don't have an answer to the brother or sister question. The refrigerator had a couple of postcards on it from someone called 'Leila,' writing to 'Uncle Lewis.' Looks like she took a trip around the Southwest last fall and wrote him a few times. Grand Canyon, petrified forest, the four corners—that kind of thing."

"Hmmm. Leila and Uncle Lewis," Barstow said. "So he had a niece with a first name. I guess that's a start."

"Well, you're in luck there," Connor said. "Because he had a file cabinet, and one thing we found in there was a will, done up by a local attorney and dated about a year ago. I only skimmed through it, but it's a simple will, and basically leaves everything to a Liela Meadows of North Granby, Connecticut."

"So that gives us the niece," Saxby said, "and if she lived in North Granby only a year ago, she shouldn't be too hard to find. With luck, she'll be the one to fill us in on any other family connections."

"There's another thing that could help with that, Chief," Connor said. "Being the organized guy that he was, he had a file labeled 'Divorce.' I only skimmed that too, but now we know his ex-wife's name, at least as of a few years ago. It's all here in this file." He patted the thick manila folder next to his notepad.

Saxby picked up the folder and leafed through it for a moment before putting it back down on the table. "Vic, would you take that please? See if you can track down this ex-wife and niece and find out whatever you can. For now, just say we're treating the case as a fatal accident in his home. No need to mention more than that. What else you got, Three? Any financial papers in that file cabinet?"

"There were some, yes," Connor said. "Usual assortment of bills and bank statements, a checkbook. Looks like he hadn't yet gotten around to the paperless route. Almost ten thousand between checking and savings, so I don't think he had any money problems. No past-due notices or anything like that, and he had IRAs with some serious money in them—like over two hundred thousand bucks."

"And it doesn't make much sense to kill someone over money in an IRA," Saxby said. "Unless you're the beneficiary. We'll have to take a closer look at all of that, but dollars to donuts the beneficiary is this niece, Leila. Any sign of anything romantic, like letters or notes from a girlfriend, maybe?"

"Nope, I haven't seen anything like that," Connor said. "I get the strong impression that he was all about his work. One thing I did find that might be a little out of character is he had a hundred-milligram package of cannabis gummies with half of one missing. The expiration date was six months ago. They're legal now, so no problem there, and we didn't see anything else related to drug use. Well, except a pretty nice bottle of scotch in the cupboard."

"One thing I think is happening a lot since pot became legal," Saxby said, "is that lots of older people who couldn't get it years ago, or were afraid of getting into trouble, are coming out of the woodwork now to give it a try. I bet he bought a pack, tried a piece, and for one reason or other didn't use the rest. Didn't like it, maybe. Anyway, something to note and probably file away. That it?"

"That's about it, as far as what we thought was significant," Connor said. "Oh, except we did gather up quite a pile of paper from around his office and lab downstairs. Reports he must have brought home or printed out, notepads full of scribbles, lots of loose papers. There's a hardcover journal and your basic weekly planner. Roy and I looked at some of it but couldn't make a whole lotta sense of it. We thought it was like trying to read through a pile of doctor's prescriptions. Might be worth a close look by someone who knows what they're looking at. We put it all in a box that's downstairs on the counter. Were you able to get a look at his office at the lab when you were out there?"

"I did, yes," Saxby said. "I was surprised at how sterile it looked. The head man, Dr. Olson, said that Forbes always kept all his notes and papers at his home, so I guess that's what we have in the box you put together. That could turn out to be very useful. Maybe we can find someone with the right background to interpret some of it for us. Okay, well, good job here. I'm headed back to the station for now. I got a message that Dr. Coyle has sent his report over, so I'll be looking that over. Let's meet up to compare notes later. See you back at the ranch."

7

It was almost five when Saxby was able to get together with Barstow and Connor in his office. The station was otherwise very quiet, with just two of the patrol officers working on paperwork at their desks. Doreen had gone home for the day, having toggled the switchboard over to the automated system. Saxby had used the microwave to heat up a cup of stale coffee left over from the last pot of the day, brewed earlier that afternoon.

"Okay, guys," Saxby said. "It's already been a long day and we've got a bunch of things to touch on, so let's get right to it. I'll pick on you first, Vic. Were you able to get anywhere with the niece or the ex-wife?"

"It's funny, Chief," Barstow said, "but oddly enough, I spoke with both of them just in the last two hours. Wasn't expecting it to be so easy to connect with them, but I'll take it. I caught Leila Meadows at her home in Connecticut and we talked for about a half-hour. She was shocked and upset by the news of course, but took it as well as can be. Turns out she isn't really Forbes' niece, because he was an only child. She's actually the ex-wife's stepdaughter from her first marriage. She's twenty-six years old and single. It's a little messy, but my understanding is that the ex-wife, a lady now going by the name of Shari Venditto, was first married to a man named Meadows, and she adopted his young daughter—Leila—from his own first marriage. Bear with me now. So, Meadows dies when Leila is a young teenager, and after a while, Shari, the widow, gets together with Lewis Forbes. That marriage lasted about eight years, with Forbes and Leila growing close, almost like father and daughter. She called him her uncle and he referred to her as his niece, out of respect for her late father. Anyway, that's how Forbes has a niece despite having no brothers or sisters."

"That's quite a story," Saxby said. "But it answers a few questions. What else did you talk about?"

"I asked her the usual questions," Barstow said. "Did she know anything about any close friends he might have had, or romantic partners, any other relatives? I had to tap dance a little bit because I told her we thought his death was accidental and I didn't want to blow the story."

"You're right, Vic," Saxby said. "I'm sorry, I shouldn't have put that requirement on you. That probably handicapped your questioning."

"I think it turned out okay, Chief," Barstow said, "because she told me she hadn't been in touch with him very much over the past two years or so. She said they were fine, but it was just a story of missed phone calls and visits talked about but not pulled off. They kept in touch a little bit now and then, like the Grand Canyon postcards Three found on the fridge. She wasn't able to tell me anything about his recent personal life, and she was unaware of any other relatives. Which, by the way, was basically the same story I got from my next call, to the ex-wife, Shari Venditto."

"Where did the 'Venditto' come from?" Connor asked. "Was she married a third time, after Forbes?"

"No, I got the impression she was done with the whole marriage thing," Barstow said. "She changed back to her maiden name—Venditto—after divorcing Forbes. She told me their parting was amicable, which was also how Leila described it. It just fizzled out. She said they sent each other Christmas or birthday cards at first, but then that fizzled out too. She also had nothing to add as far as his social life. He was mostly all about whatever research he was working on, is how she put it. His parents were long gone, and as we've already established, there were no siblings."

"Okay, so, it doesn't look like there's any kind of family angle to this," Saxby said. "And we haven't heard much about him yet, but what we have heard seems to agree that he was a loner who cared most about his work, at least over the past few years. Anything else, Vic?"

"That's it as far as family goes," Barstow said. "Leila Meadows is going to plan to come down next week to start going through his stuff and handle what needs to be handled. I asked her to let me know when she figures out her plans and I'll try to coordinate with her. Aside from that, I started looking at the box full of reports and notes and all that we took from the apartment, but I didn't get to spend much time on it. I know I'm not dumb, but I didn't understand much of what I was looking at anyway. What about asking Dr. Olson, or one of the other people we talked to today to look at it and explain it to us?"

"It might come to that, Vic," Saxby said, "but hold that thought for the time being. We don't know where this is going yet, and I'd like to keep it a little bit compartmentalized for now. We need to remember that someone out there at the lab could be a suspect. Let me think about that one for a while and I'll get back to you. Now over to you, Three. Have you had time to read Dr. Coyle's full report?"

"I did," Connor said. "It pretty much stuck to what you told us from when the doctor stopped by your house last night, plus a little bit more. Aside from Dr. Forbes, there was one other person there with him Sunday night. At some point, when Forbes' back was turned—walking away possibly—the unknown assailant grabbed the Bunsen burner by the shaft and used it to hit Forbes once on the head with a lot of force. Forbes then spun around and fell backwards, hitting the back of his head against the edge of the counter. About where the neck meets the skull. He then fell the rest of the way to the cement floor, landing in a prone position. The report estimates that he was out cold at that time and died within a very few minutes. The assailant, by the way, must have had the presence of mind to try to wipe any prints off the Bunsen burner. The lab found a few fragments, but nothing clear or usable."

"He wiped it for prints, interesting," Saxby said. "I'm just saying that because one of my theories is that the assailant grabbed the burner and hit him with it on impulse. In the heat of the moment, but then panicked and got out of there when he saw how it all turned out."

"I get you, Chief," Barstow said. "You mean like, 'Yeah,

we were arguing and I lost my temper. I grabbed the thing and swung it at him but I never meant to kill him.'"

"Exactly. That's what I've been thinking might have happened," Saxby said. "But if it was something like that, it's odd that he was cool enough to grab a towel or use his shirt to wipe the thing for prints."

"You know, maybe it's crazy," Connor said, "but with everyone growing up with all the shows on TV and the movies, we've all seen the killer wipe the weapon down a million times. Whether it's a gun, a knife, a candlestick, a Bunsen burner—whatever. I'm just saying that idea to grab a towel or a napkin and wipe off the weapon is something that's imprinted on all of us from a young age, for better or worse."

"Not a crazy thought, Three," Saxby said. "You might be on to something there. He didn't pick up all those papers or notebooks, yet he thought to do that one thing. Food for thought. Wasn't there a footprint you found also? Where are we with that?"

"Doesn't look like it's going to be much help," Connor said, "apart from showing that someone other than Forbes, probably a man, was there with him at the time he was killed, which is something we already know. The material that made the print did include some of the brick dust from just outside the door, but the print itself is only a partial, and too blurry to give us the size or brand of shoe. It appears to be a full-sized man's shoe, maybe a size ten or larger. Nothing very distinctive."

"Okay, well, that's too bad," Saxby said, "but at least it helps steer us towards some kind of attack rather than an accident, so it wasn't entirely useless."

"I just had a thought," Barstow said, "about all those papers that were scattered around on the floor and the counter, like stuff he was reading or working on."

"Right. That's the box of stuff you started to look at earlier," Saxby said.

"Yeah, that's what I mean," Barstow said. "And we were talking about how he had taken a minute to wipe down the Bunsen burner, but hadn't tried to take all those papers. I'm just thinking out loud here, but if someone *had* taken those papers, wouldn't that imply that this was somehow related to his work?"

"That's a good thought, Vic," Saxby said. "I'd agree that would make things point in the work direction. Keep in mind, though, that someone, in fact, might have taken something, if they knew what they were looking for and found it quickly enough. They might have taken this or that and left the rest. Maybe they didn't, but in any case, whatever we have is what they didn't take. Anything else on Dr. Coyle's report or the crime scene, Three?"

"Nothing worth much as far as I can tell," Connor said. "Aside from the footprint, the Bunsen burner, and the fact that there was obviously a fatal attack, we don't have anything else that points to a particular person being Forbes' visitor the other night. No indications of robbery and no signs of forced entry. Whoever it was who came to see him and ended up killing him was probably someone he knew and trusted enough to let into his home."

"Right, right. Whatever the fight was came a little later," Saxby said. "So, from this point on, we are considering this a murder investigation. Vic, would you please give the ex-wife and the niece who isn't a niece a call back to tell them that? We're working on it and we'll update them at a later date, etcetera. You know what to say. I've already talked with the county detectives, and they've assigned Detective Bill Hagen to the case. I've worked with Bill in the past and he's a good guy, but he's going to be hands-off unless we need specific help. They're up to their necks with some big drug cases going on up in the north of the county. So, by all means, we call him if we need him to expedite lab work, get a search warrant, or whatever, and I will send him updates. Otherwise, this is gonna be our show. Now, tomorrow is a new day. Three, first thing, would you please start setting up the big board in the conference room with anything we have so far. Crime scene, ex-wife, names of co-workers—all the usual stuff. I know we don't have much yet, but let's get off to an organized start. Vic, now that we know what we're dealing with, I think we need to speak specifically with the two people at the lab who worked most closely with Forbes: Arthur Hill and Windsor Bell. I'd like to hold off on Hill just a little longer, but I'd like you to focus on a chat with Bell tomorrow. See if you can dig a little deeper into her work relationship with Forbes and see where that goes. It's not that we think she's a suspect, more that we're looking for an insider's take on the situation. Make sense?"

"Yes, got it, no problem at all," Barstow said. "But, of those two, Hill and Bell, he's the one who fits Dr. Coyle's description of our likely assailant, right? Meaning, men about six feet, or big, strong women. I wouldn't call Bell a big, strong woman. Why is it you want to wait on Hill? Is it that feeling we both had when we interviewed him?"

"That's something, but mostly I'd like to get a little

further along before shaking that tree," Saxby said. He paused for a moment, scratching the top of his head. "We were talking a minute ago about if this is work-related, and I'm finding it hard to think that it's not. I'm thinking about Forbes and what happened at his place. No robbery, no love triangle, no sign of a drug deal. Just a man who seems to be mostly about his work. Which makes me think of his work, which makes me think of the people he worked with. And I know the doctor's description of a likely assailant applies to something like eighty percent of all men, but it only applies to a much smaller percentage of the people who work at that lab, and precisely one of the people he worked most closely with—Arthur Hill. So yeah, that's barely enough to call him a person of interest at the moment but it's not nothing. Just sharing my thought process and keeping an open mind.

"You know, come to think of it, when you contact Bell, see if you can do it on the QT and meet her for a coffee or something outside the office. Remember, 'potential witness' is all any of these people are at the moment."

Saxby looked at his watch. "Tomorrow is another day, but first, I haven't been to the Mug in almost a week and I'm overdue. I'll be meeting up with Angela there after dinner, about eight. If either of you feel like joining, drinks are on me. If not, get some rest and take care of yourselves. For the first time in nowhere near long enough, we've got another murderer in town."

8

The crowd at the Ugly Mug Tavern was characteristically sparse for a Tuesday night in October, and Saxby had no trouble getting his usual booth. In short order, the bartender came around from behind the bar and set down a double bourbon on the rocks.

"Well, thanks, Cody," Saxby said, with an exaggerated look of surprise. "I was just starting to think about what to have, but now you've saved me the trouble. That looks perfect."

"I hope you don't think I'm being too presumptuous," Cody said, "but when you came in I saw you wearing a look I've seen before and I figured this was the ticket. It's a Blanton's Single Barrel. I almost fell over when our distributor dropped off a whole case, and I set a couple bottles aside for you. If you like it, I'll drop one off at your house."

Saxby, who had sipped the potent amber liquid while Cody was talking, said: "Mmmm, 'good stuff' is putting it mildly, though 'nectar of the gods' might be a bit too flowery for bourbon. Anyway, it's delicious, and I'll take you up on that offer of a bottle. Just leave it on the porch if nobody's home. Will you join me?"

"I'd better get back behind the bar," Cody said, "but I'll pour myself a taste. Quality control, you know. Any responsible bartender needs to make sure the top-shelf booze is good enough. Are you on a secret mission tonight, or shall I tell Angela you're here? She's up in the office finishing up with the orders."

"Yeah, please, tell her I'm here," Saxby said. "She's expecting me."

"Got it, then," Cody said. "I'll tell her there's some guy down here drinking all the expensive booze like he owns the joint."

He went back behind the bar, where he picked up the phone to call the upstairs office. Saxby's fiancée and long-time main squeeze, Angela Andrews, emerged from a doorway across the room a few minutes later. Saxby stood up from the booth to get a big hug and a quick kiss before they both sat down.

"That's the best thing that's happened to me all day," Saxby said. "Are you sure you can break away from your managerial duties for a while?"

"Absolutely. There's work to do," Angela said, "but no more that's got to get done tonight." She made a quick scan of the room, turning to check that the booths on either side of them were empty. "How about you? Anything new you can talk about with that guy they found yesterday?"

Saxby looked into his drink and stirred the remaining ice cubes for a moment. "Sorry, Ang. Didn't mean to be dramatic there. It's just that … well, I hate that you've got to hear about all the terrible stuff I have to deal with."

"Hey, listen to me," Angela said. "I signed up for this. Nobody's twisting my arm. I know you've got Vic and Three, and the others, but sometimes you need to be able to vent to someone who isn't a cop. That's part of my job. I mean, sure, I run this place, and help with the Harbor House and the other places, but another part of my job is being around to listen to you and hearing the gory details. You got me? So, let's hear it, Chief Saxby."

"Geez, you can be a tough broad sometimes," Saxby said. He caught Cody's eye over behind the bar and signaled for a refill on his drink and added his standard 'get Angela a glass of wine' gesture. "But as usual, you're also right. Anyway, I don't really have many gory details, but okay, I'll fill you in."

Relating an abbreviated version of the Forbes case to her took up the next fifteen minutes, interrupted by Cody bringing over their drinks and then a waitress dropping off a basket of fries. Being a long-time fan of all the serial killer shows on cable TV, Angela's eyes grew wide when Saxby told her that the case had officially become a murder investigation.

"I can't believe it," Angela said, after a conspiratorial look around the room. "I grew up here and I can't think of anything like this going on before, you know, that thing with the mugs and all that…" She gestured to the beer mugs hanging all over the ceiling, which had figured prominently in a sensational multiple-murder case from several years back. "And then those other two cases that came after—it's crazy. Is this going to be every year now?"

"Oh, come on. Now you're the one being dramatic," Saxby said. "This is not a TV show. We don't know what it is yet, but there's no reason to think it's any kind of a big thing. I know one thing, though, and that is that we'll figure it out."

"That's it right there, sweets," Angela said. "You'll figure it out. That's why you're the police chief. You know, I had a thought about something you said a while back. You said something about a pile of stuff your people collected from his apartment, and you said how nobody could tell what it was."

"That's right, pretty much," Saxby said. "It's a scientist making notes for himself or for other scientists I guess, and it's full of jargon and abbreviations that wouldn't make sense to we non-scientists. I was thinking of asking Dr. Coyle to look at it, but I hate to bother him. He's always got so much on his plate."

"Or on his slab, you might say," Angela said, with the closest thing to a devilish grin that Saxby had seen in ages. "But seriously, I have a brilliant idea. Call Mark Allen. I caught his radio show last Friday. He had a guy on who was some kind of fancy scientist. I don't remember his name, but what I do remember is that he had written a book about how fish traveling all around are being affected by global warming. He talked a lot about the Gulf Stream, and big fish like marlin and tuna and sharks."

"That does sound interesting," Saxby said. "But was this guy a local person?"

"No, I don't think so," Angela said. "But the reason I'm saying this is, he mentioned that after all the work of publishing his new book, he was taking a few weeks off to relax. You should talk to Mark Allen and see if the guy's still around. Maybe he's staying in Cape May. You could ask him to look through all that stuff and tell you what it means. That way, those other people at the place on the beach wouldn't need to know what you were up to. What do you think?"

"You know what, I think that's a damn good idea," Saxby said. He glanced at his watch. "Mark's an early-to-bed, early-to-rise kind of guy. I'll wait till morning to call him. Really good idea though, Ang. Hmmm, I had offered Vic and Three a drink if they felt like stopping in, but I guess they had other stuff going on."

"They might just be camped out on the couch watching a horror movie," Angela said. "Everyone needs their own 'veg time.' Anyway, it's getting late, and I was hoping you were planning to take me home soon."

"Well, I'm shocked, future Mrs. Saxby. Are you hinting at something?"

"Probably. So, let's get outta here, shall we? I'll get my jacket and I'll drive. Leave a nice tip, Chief."

9

Saxby started the next day early, making a few calls over his toast and coffee. The first was to Mark Allen, local radio host, newspaper columnist, amateur historian, and general man-about-town. He had helped Saxby and the department on several occasions in the past, and seemed somehow to always know what was going on in town. Saxby considered him a reliable confidant.

"Well, good morning, Tate," Allen said, having answered on the third ring. "You sure are up with the roosters today. Just fifteen minutes earlier and you would've been rousting me out of my beauty sleep. What's up?"

"Morning, Mark," Saxby said. "Sorry about the early call, but not all that sorry, because I know you get up early. I need to run something by you and ask a few questions. It's not an emergency, but is fairly urgent. Have you got time this morning?"

"I guess you're in luck," Allen said, "because I was toying with the idea of going out for breakfast. Now it'll taste even better because you're buying. How does the Ocean View in thirty minutes grab you? Call it eight o'clock."

"That's perfect, Mark, thanks a lot," Saxby said. "I'll forego any more coffee until we meet. We should be able to get a quiet table there. See you in thirty."

"Roger that," Allen said, ending the call.

Saxby's next call was to Sergeant Barstow, catching her as she was just arriving at the police station.

"Hey, Chief, what's up?" Barstow said. "I'm just getting in. Are you here in your office?"

"No, Vic, and good morning to you," Saxby said. "I'm still home, but I'm on to something this morning and I need to meet with Mark Allen to hash it out."

He took a few minutes to tell her about the scientist Angela had heard on the radio show, and how he was hoping to be able to connect with the man.

"That sounds promising, Chief," Barstow said. "And here I first thought you were just using all of this as an excuse to go out for breakfast. I hope you can get hold of the guy."

"Very funny, Vic," Saxby said. "You're going to try to catch up with Windsor Bell today, that right?"

"Yes, that's at the top of my list for this morning," Barstow said. "I have her private cell, and I'll see if I can get her out of the office. If she won't cooperate, I'll bring out the old rubber hose."

"I'm glad you maintain your sense of humor with everything that's going on," Saxby said. "I'm sure you'll handle it just fine. I'll catch up with you a little later and we'll go over everything."

Fifteen minutes later, Saxby met Mark Allen in the parking lot of the Ocean View, directly across from the beach, and they walked in together.

"Well, if it isn't Mark Allen with our famous police chief," the hostess said, flashing them a bright smile. "Are you joining us for breakfast this morning?"

"Yes, Grace, that would be nice," Saxby said. "Mark and I need to have a sort of breakfast meeting. Can we get a table with some privacy? Maybe in the back room?"

"Certainly, Chief," she said. "There's nobody else in there right now, and I'll make sure to not seat anyone else near you."

She led them to a four-top against the wall in a room where the other dozen or so tables were empty. A young waitress soon took their orders and brought coffee, leaving a thermos on the table.

"I know you've got something serious you want to talk about," Allen said, "and I'm guessing it has to do with the dead man you found the other morning, so feel free to get right to it. We can bullshit about the parking problems in town and everything else over some stronger drinks another time soon."

Over their coffee and continuing after the food arrived, Saxby told Allen about what the police had so far on the Lewis Forbes case. They talked about the most common reasons that one person tends to kill another, and how romance, drugs, or involvement with major crimes in general didn't seem to apply to Forbes.

"It wasn't robbery and there wasn't any forced entry,"

Saxby said. "He had to have been attacked, and killed, ultimately, by someone he knew. Far as we can see, the only people he associated with are the ones he worked with out at that research lab on the beach. And I'm having trouble with the idea that the work they did could have been a reason for violence. Or any of those scientists being involved for that matter."

"Hmmm, yeah, I see what you're saying," Allen said. "Killing someone, or even banging them on the head, is serious stuff. Tell me again about what they're doing out there at the lab."

"Well, they're working on different projects," Saxby said. "But Forbes, along with two of the others, was focused on finding ways that marine life—mollusks, actually—could be used to cure disease in humans. Apparently, he was really hot on the trail for that."

"Mollusks, you say," Allen said. "Hmmm. Did you catch what type?"

"Yeah, scallops," Saxby said. "From what Dr. Olson told me, Forbes and the others had a theory that some part of the scallops found offshore around here could have something in them that could help treat Alzheimer's disease. They thought it could be a really big deal."

"And, as I'm sure you know," Allen said, "there are vast scallop fields along the continental shelf off South Jersey."

"Right. I know that," Saxby said. "So, if it were to turn out that some of our local scallops had an enzyme or protein or whatever, that could treat disease, medical people would be very excited about that, but other people wouldn't be so happy."

"Exactly. Like scallop fisherman, for example," Allen

said. "They'd be worried about the government coming in and hurting their business by protecting the scallop beds. You know, that would be a tough one to work out, because that's a substantial food crop and a big bucks business. Scallops are expensive. I guess it would be ideal if the part of the scallop that was useful to medicine wasn't the same part that people like to eat."

"That might help," Saxby said, "but then we'd still have a huge problem, because scallop harvesting is a hustle business. Right out there on the ship they cut out the meat—you know, that round blob of scallop meat—and toss the rest overboard. Their income hinges on working around the clock and working fast. Scallop people would flip out if they couldn't do that anymore."

"I think the idea we're circling around here," Allen said, "is that there are probably any number of people out there with their fingers crossed, hoping this scallop research doesn't pan out."

"Agreed. So then, if on a scale of one to ten, 'fingers crossed' is a one," Saxby said, "then I guess attacking or killing someone would be a ten. The problem with that is, I can see people waiting nervously and hoping the research doesn't go anywhere, okay, sure. But even if you were enough of an angry nutcase to attack a scientist over it, that just doesn't make sense to me. What good is attacking one scientist going to do? Doesn't add up. There's got to be more to this."

"I agree with you on that, Tate," Allen said, "and I bet I know what it is. Offshore wind. There, I said it. Offshore wind. Damn. I should have thought of that right off the bat. Sure as I'm sitting here, Tate, that's it. I know you probably don't have much time to read the paper, but were you aware that there's been a major effort to build a huge wind farm off the coast of Cape May County?"

"No. I didn't know about that. I mean, I'm aware that those project ideas come and go," Saxby said, "and I know it's a big political football, but it's not something I follow very much. I think the gist of it is that the renewable energy people want wind farms and lots of other people are always trying to stop them. I assume the fossil-fuel people hate the idea, and then there's all the NIMBYs up and down the coast."

"You've got the main points down pretty well," Allen said. "So, a lot of the recent fuss around here, what you've been missing, is that going back about a year, a company called Trans-Oceanic Wind had been angling for approval to build a huge wind farm a few miles offshore. They're talking about thirty or forty turbines. You know, wind-mills. The approval comes with a renewable energy research grant from the feds, and it's big money, like a hundred million or more."

"Whew, yeah. That is serious money," Saxby said. His memory immediately jumped back to another murder case he had worked on with Chief Martin Banks of North Wildwood. There was one afternoon when they had learned of the huge amounts of money potentially at stake in that case. The two of them had realized at the same moment what kind of money that was—"the killin' kind." "What happened to Lewis Forbes is part of something big and dirty, is where I'm leaning. That's what my gut's telling me. I think he may have been a pawn in some kind of big-money game, but what game is that? I mean, sure, this whole wind farm thing could fit the bill, but I'm missing what that has to do with Forbes or the work he was doing."

"Well, you're the cop here, Tate. I'm just spouting ideas, but yes," Allen said. "Whoever attacked the guy did it for a reason, right? And if you don't see a simple reason, like drugs or a spurned lover or whatever, then I have to agree with you that it's probably a more complex reason. If you're thinking it might be related to the work he was doing, then you're going to have to think about both sides —meaning, who would want that work to be successful as well as who would want it to fail."

"Forbes and the other scientists are trying to find ways that scallops could somehow help treat Alzheimer's disease," Saxby said. "I'm having a hard time thinking of people wanting that to fail."

"That's because you're a decent, caring person, Tate," Allen said. "The idea of someone wanting it to fail is distasteful. But set that aside for a minute and think of it in terms of that really big money we talked about. If the research was successful, the government might step in to protect the scallop beds. We talked about scallop people. We can assume they wouldn't like it, but the biggest loser would probably be Trans-Oceanic Wind, who wouldn't get their wind farm."

"I got ya," Saxby said. "And the oil and gas people would *want* the research to succeed, because then, for the same reasons, the wind farm wouldn't get built."

"There's a few different angles to this, to be sure," Allen said. "You know who you should talk to? You should talk to Brewster Atwater. He's the president of Garden State Shellfish, which is a kind of umbrella company for a bunch of New Jersey fisheries, including scallop operations. I wouldn't say I know him, but I met him once a few years ago, and he seemed like an outgoing guy. I believe he lives in Wildwood, but his office is right here in the harbor."

"I'll check him out and probably look him up," Saxby said, scribbling on a pocket notepad. "Thanks for the idea. Maybe he could help me get a pulse on the whole thing."

"He might be a good source to start with if you can get in to see him," Allen said. "If I think of anyone else, I'll let you know."

The waitress dropped off a check and cleared the last of the dishes. Allen poured out a last half-cup of coffee while Saxby straightened out a few bills.

"Was that it or was there anything else you wanted to ask me about?" Allen said.

"Ah, yes, there was something else," Saxby said. "Lewis Forbes had sort of a combo lab and office at his place. When we went through it, we put together a box of all sorts of notepads, reports, ideas written on scraps of paper —it's a whole pile of material that's mostly Greek to us. We thought it would make sense to find some scientist or doctor to look through it and tell us what it all means. I mean, without having to involve his manager or the other scientists where he worked. Angela told me last night that you had a marine biologist or someone like that on your show last week, and she thought he might still be here in town. If he was still around, I thought it wouldn't hurt to ask if he could help us out."

"Well, he is still in town," Allen said, "and I bet he'd be happy to help. Super nice guy. Clemson Colson's his name. Doctor of something, but I don't remember exactly what.

He's an expert on the Gulf Stream and Atlantic weather patterns. I'll dig up his info and email it to you as soon as I get home."

"Great, thanks a lot, Mark," Saxby said, as they walked to their cars. "I appreciate being able to bounce all this stuff off someone else. My officers all are fantastic, and I'm lucky to have them, but sometimes it's good to get a point of view from someone who doesn't carry a badge."

"And who can keep his mouth shut, right?" Allen said, with a laugh. "You're welcome, Chief. Watch for that email."

It had been a long breakfast meeting, but Saxby thought the time had been well spent. He was working in his office when Sergeant Barstow got in about an hour later. She knocked on the open door, notebook in hand. "Okay time to catch up, Chief?" She waited for Saxby's gesture before taking a seat.

"I had a good meeting with Mark Allen," Saxby said. "Very interesting. Gave me some ideas. But first, were you able to get together with Windsor Bell?"

"I did, yes," Barstow said, "and I think that was a good meeting too. I definitely picked up that she was glad for the chance to talk away from her office, and she had a lot to say. When I confirmed that Forbes had been violently attacked, it was like the floodgates opened and all kinds of stuff came out."

"Are you saying she had ideas about who would have wanted to hurt him? Or hurt them?" Saxby said.

"Yes, both. Him and them," Barstow said. "In an abstract way at least. She told me that she's thought for a long time that there must be all kinds of powerful people who don't want their research to be successful. They were trying to find a treatment, or a cure even, for Alzheimer's, and she was getting a feeling more and more that someone might try to stop them. The only thing anywhere close to specific was when she mentioned something about a wind farm. I didn't know this, but apparently there's a company trying to get approval to build a lot of those huge wind mill things off the coast. She had the idea that there might be some powerful people out there somewhere—she didn't know who, just 'powerful people'—intent on messing with their research to somehow affect this wind farm idea. I didn't see the connection there and when I pressed her on it she didn't have any details. Actually, I had the feeling she might know more but decided to clam up for whatever reason. But now this happens with Forbes, and she's starting to think the thing she was worried about is really happening. I gotta tell you, Chief, there was a time or two when she was talking that I started to think she was a little flaky, like she might start to talk about chemtrails or the faked moon landing any minute, but in the end I decided that wasn't fair. I mean, she has a doctorate in marine biology after all. She's about as far from dumb as a person can get. I think we should take her very seriously."

"What a morning, Vic," Saxby said. "Because what you're telling me you talked about with this Dr. Bell is a lot like the conversation I just had with Mark Allen. He brought up this wind farm stuff to me also. I guess I need to read the paper more often."

Saxby took a few minutes and did his best to relate the details of the breakfast meeting with Allen and his ideas about how to move forward with the investigation.

"If it turns out that our local scallops could be useful in medicine," Saxby said, "it's a reasonable bet the government will put the kibosh on any wind farm off the coast, because a wind farm would damage the scallop beds too much. Also, we already know the oil and gas companies are trying to do anything they can to slow down research and investment into wind energy."

"And let's not forget the developers who think a wind farm off the coast would ruin the view and make it harder to sell condos," Barstow said. "I don't get that myself, but I know it's a thing with some people."

"You're right," Saxby said. "But here's the problem with all of this, and this is something that makes my head hurt. See, we're talking about all the people who would benefit from *stopping* the wind farm. In other words, all the people who would hope for the scallop cure to pan out. But when I start to think that maybe Forbes was killed to somehow slow down the research, that's when it stops making sense. Those people we're talking about—oil and gas and all that —should be rooting for the research to succeed, right? So, why was he killed? My conclusion then, as logic dictates, has to be that Forbes was killed for some reason other than someone trying to slow down or stop the research."

"Well, he damn sure wasn't killed to speed it up," Barstow said.

"Out of the mouths of babes," Saxby said. "Your comment follows the logic, but you know, it's also funny, because, crazy as that might sound on the surface, I'm not so sure right now, Vic. There's a tiny spark of an idea way in the back of my head. It's just a germ, but if it grows into anything that makes sense, I'll let you know. Meanwhile, we've talked about who would want to stop the wind farm. How about the other side of the coin? Who would want it to be built?"

"Well, the obvious answer is the company that wants to build the thing," Barstow said. "Do we know who that is?"

"I do, since breakfast," Saxby said, "because Mark Allen told me. Trans-Oceanic Wind is the name of the company. I was just starting to look that up when you came in, so I don't know much yet, other than it's a French company, headed up by a French woman. Apparently, they're one of the biggest players around the Atlantic Basin."

"And they'd stand to cash in big time if the project got a green light," Barstow said. "Millions and millions. Then, aside from the actual company, there's the usual green energy groups, the anti-fossil fuel people. I see them being happy if the wind farm was being built, but not getting rich from it."

"Agreed," Saxby said. "And—just kicking ideas around here—if anyone were going to take criminal action to help the wind farm get built, that would probably be whoever stood to gain millions of dollars. Trans-Oceanic Wind, most likely. We'll need to take a close look at them. Anyway, let's move on. How did it end up with this Bell lady?"

"I have her personal number and she said she'd be happy to talk again," Barstow said. "I definitely got the impression that she had more to say but was holding back for some reason. I didn't want to push too hard and antagonize her, but I think there might be something there for future conversations."

"Okay, good. Maybe later you and I can meet with her privately," Saxby said. "Aside from that, there are several things we need to do next. One of them is to start talking to people in the area who are big in the fossil fuel or the scallop industries. Bearing in mind the puzzle we've already discussed. That could help give us a sense of the overall climate and where to go from there. Mark Allen suggested I start with a man by the name of Brewster Atwater, who heads up a powerful group of New Jersey seafood companies. He lives in the area, so I'll start with him. Another thing we need to take action on right away is that box of papers we collected from Forbes' place. Mark gave me the number of a marine scientist who was on his radio show last week. He thinks the guy's still in town for a while. I'll try to contact him and see if I can get him to read through that box and help us understand what we have. Clemson Colson is his name."

"I'll put the box back together and bring it in here for you," Barstow said. "I've already made copies of the appointment book and a few other things, so I'll make some time to look at that myself later."

"Good plan," Saxby said. "Get that to me as soon as you can. I'll make the calls to try to set up a meeting with him and also with Atwater, the Garden State Shellfish guy. Let's you and I plan to compare notes later."

10

I t was early afternoon by the time Saxby managed to break free of his desk and drive over to Brewster Atwater's office in the marina area of town. The building looked to be of recent construction, though done up in the style of a classic New England seashore house, with well-weathered cedar shingles all around and a pair of white-trimmed dormer windows looking out from the second floor. He parked the car amongst several others and went inside, finding himself in a comfortably appointed reception area where a professionally-dressed thirtyish woman worked at a large, modern desk.

"Good afternoon. You must be Chief Saxby," the receptionist said. "Is that correct?"

"Yes, that's correct," Saxby said, glancing at his watch. "Tate Saxby, Cape May Police. Here for Mr. Atwater. I think I spoke with you on the phone. I'm afraid I've gotten here a few minutes early."

"Oh, that's fine," she said. "Mr. Atwater is just finishing up with his last appointment."

Whether the young lady was psychic or just an excellent secretary would remain a mystery to Saxby, but at that moment the door to the inner office opened. A tall, slim, silver-haired man held the door for an expensively dressed woman to come through. As Saxby took in the two of them, the idea flashed across his mind that the man and his lady visitor had walked right out of a magazine ad for Ralph Lauren Polo. *Hmmm, no. She's more Chanel. Anyway, money.*

Recovering quickly from a hint of surprise at seeing someone else in the outer office, the man came right up to Saxby with a broad smile and an outstretched hand. Saxby guessed the man to be four or five inches north of six feet.

"Hello. I'm Brewster Atwater. Good to meet you, Chief Saxby. I hope you weren't waiting long."

"Oh no, I've only been here a minute," Saxby said. "Tate Saxby. Pleased to meet you as well. I hope I'm not interrupting anything."

"Oh no, you're not interrupting," Atwater said, "I've just been catching up with my friend and occasional associate here, Miss…"

"Duval. Camille Duval," the lady said, cutting Atwater off and thrusting her hand out to Saxby. "I am pleased to meet the chief of police of this lovely town."

"Pleased to meet you as well, Miss Duval," Saxby said. "I hope you're able to find time to enjoy your visit."

"I will try to do that, thank you," Duval said. "But right now, I'm afraid I must rush to my next appointment. Good seeing you again, Brewster, and good meeting you, Mr. Saxby."

With a smile and nod of her head, she went out.

"Well, Chief Saxby, why don't you come in and sit down and we'll see how I can help you," Atwater said. He followed Saxby into the office, closing the door behind them.

He gestured to a small sitting area off to one side of the spacious office, and they took seats separated by a low coffee table.

"That was an interesting lady," Saxby said. "German, I imagine? Based on the accent."

"You know, I hardly notice it anymore, but that could be. I seem to remember her telling me once that she was largely raised by a German nurse," Atwater said. "You know how those privileged families are. Well then, to what do I owe the honor of a visit from the chief of police? My secretary said something about a case you were working on and that you thought I might be able to help in some way. I'm sure you can count on me to try."

"I appreciate that, Mr. Atwater," Saxby said. "And yes, my department is working on a case that came up just a few days ago in town. A man was attacked and killed late Sunday evening in what appears to have been some sort of confrontation that escalated to the point of violence. An argument that got out of hand perhaps. We're in the early stages of the investigation, but it's starting to appear to me that this argument, or this attack, could be part of some-thing much bigger. I want to stress 'could be,' because, as I've mentioned, we're in the early stages with this. Let me take a few minutes to give you the background as concisely as I can..."

"This is fascinating," Atwater said, after Saxby had related the basics of the Forbes case. "And of course, very tragic. Obviously. It's terrible what happened to that poor man. Forbes, I think you said his name was. So, if I'm hearing you correctly, Chief Saxby, you're interested in the possibility that this ... the attack on him, could somehow center around some entity wanting to stop the wind farm from being built. And you've come to talk to me because, I suppose, I represent an organization—one of many, I might add—that could be perceived as wanting to stop the wind farm from being built. Am I in the right ballpark?"

Tate Saxby had long been a man who appreciated clear and direct communication, and was both a bit surprised and more than a little pleased with Atwater's straightforward comments.

"I certainly haven't come here today to accuse you of anything, Mr. Atwater, but as long as we're speaking directly, then yes, you're in the right ballpark. I'd like to stress, though, that this idea of some kind of linkage to wind farm construction is just that at the moment—an idea. It's a possibility that came up previously in speaking with other people about the case, and I thought it was worthy of consideration. Look, Mr. Atwater, the fact is that somebody attacked Lewis Forbes and that attack resulted in his death. One of our avenues of investigation is his work, or his work-life. I'm sure you can understand that one of our main questions would be something like 'what was he working on, and who might stand to benefit from the success, or lack of success, of that work?' When I ask myself 'Who would be against the building of a wind farm?' one of the first things that comes to mind is fishermen, or at least the kind who depend on being able to drag the sea floor."

"Like scallopers," Atwater said. "Yes, they would stand to lose a lot of their fishable area if a wind farm was built off the coast and the scallop beds were designated as off-limits for seafood harvesting purposes. It's reasonable to think that local scallop operations could be devastated."

"I understand that," Saxby said. "And as far as other types of fishing off New Jersey, I don't know enough about that to know how those people would be affected. Actually, that's more to the point of why I wanted to run all of this by you."

"The impact could be great across the seafood industry," Atwater said. "Not only from a wind farm being in operation, but perhaps even more, the extremely disruptive and potentially years-long installation process. The impact of that would be enormous. The construction and anchoring of those gigantic concrete bases can be very damaging to the marine environment. But look, Mr. Saxby—excuse me, Chief Saxby—I'm happy to help however I can, but maybe I can save you some time, because I'm sure you're as busy as I am. Yes, it's true that there are thousands of people in the state, including many who might be affiliated with my organization, whose livelihoods would be hurt if this wind project goes through. Some people would have to find new jobs. Others might decide to leave the area for opportunities elsewhere. Sure, that would happen, but that kind of disruption can happen in any industry. Our people aren't thugs. We don't go around beating up people who disagree with us. We know change is going to happen, whether or not it's to our personal benefit."

"I appreciate your candor," Saxby said. "And I'll reiterate

that at this point all I'm doing is trying to learn about the effect the wind farm might have on various concerns."

"Someone has been killed, and you're looking at anyone who could be seen as having a motive," Atwater said. "That seems very reasonable to me."

"As you correctly point out," Saxby said, "we're looking at, or looking *for*, I should say, anyone who might have a motive to want to attack Lewis Forbes. Possibly as a way to stop or slow his research, but you see, that's where I run into a wall. A conundrum. Because the thing is, if you wanted to stop the wind farm, you would want the research to be successful. And the opposite is true if you wanted the wind farm to be built. Does that make sense Mr. Atwater?"

"Well, first, let me say that I'm glad I'm not the detective on this case," Atwater said. "But yes, that does seem logical. For example, to continue on your thread, if I, representing the fishing industry, did *not* want a wind farm to be built, it follows that I *would* want this research to succeed. It further follows therefore, that it wouldn't make sense for me to try to hurt this scientist. It is as you say, Chief Saxby, a conundrum. But isn't it also possible that he was killed for some reason other than to somehow affect his research?"

"That's absolutely possible, and we'll continue to look at it from all angles," Saxby said. He stood up. "Well, I think I've taken enough of your time for now, Mr. Atwater. You've given me a bit of a feel for what I was looking for. I appreciate your meeting with me on such short notice."

"My pleasure, Chief Saxby," Atwater said. "I wish you success with your investigation, and I hope I've been of some help. Please do contact me if you have more questions. My secretary can always find me."

They shook hands and Atwater walked Saxby out to the reception area, where the secretary gave him a card. Outside, Saxby got into his cruiser, where he sat for a minute, slipping into a reverie. A pleasant memory came to him from … somewhere, but he didn't know where. He was at a quiet restaurant, a nautical-looking place at the seashore, having dinner with his late mother. Maybe it was at the Harbor House, but that part of the memory eluded him. *Strange. Why now?* The sound of a horn honking in nearby traffic brought him back to the present, and he started the car. As he pulled out of the lot, he noted that the recent-year dark blue Jaguar that had been there when he arrived was now gone.

Saxby's next appointment was with Dr. Clemson Colson, the marine biologist who was vacationing in town after having recently been a guest on Mark Allen's radio show. When Saxby had called him a few hours earlier, Colson had given his address and told Saxby to drop by any time that afternoon. The directions brought Saxby to a unit on the top floor of one of the condo buildings along the beachfront. Colson answered the door promptly and saw Saxby to a table in the small but nicely appointed eat-in kitchen, with dark cherry cabinets and granite countertops to match. Saxby refused the other man's offer of coffee.

"Thanks very much," Saxby said. "It smells good, but my breakfast with Mark Allen went into overtime this morning. I think we overdid it on the coffee. Mark spoke highly of you, and I'm grateful that you could fit me into your schedule today."

"Well, I'll tell you, my schedule at the moment is mostly blank," Colson said with a laugh. "I've been all up and down the coast now since my book came out in June, and I'm just about beat. This is the first I've been in Cape May for years, and it just struck me as a great place to take a break. I got a great deal on this rental, and I've got a few days before my wife shows up to join me. So, it looks like you've got some good timing. Mark said you might like some help with interpreting some kind of scientific papers? I see you've brought a box with you."

"You have that right, yes," Saxby said. "I think that to start, it would be a good idea for me to take ten minutes and give you some background, if that's okay."

"Good. I think that makes a lot of sense," Colson said. "The more I know about where you're coming from on this, and what you're looking for, the more likely it is that I'll be able to help out. Let's hear it."

Having summarized the key points of the Lewis Forbes case less than an hour earlier for Brewster Atwater, Saxby found it easy to give Colson a similar version, touching, he hoped, on all the key points, adding, this time, that he had met with Atwater earlier.

"One of the main things about this," Saxby said, having finished the general summary of the case, "is that we don't know what his state of mind was regarding his work. What I mean is, did he think he was close to a breakthrough? Was he excited about some new progress? Or was he deflated by something he'd found. And certainly, is there any indication of conflicts, or disagreements with the people he worked with? These papers may or may not answer any of those questions, but your unbiased read could be very helpful. As someone who speaks the language, if I may. We'll pay you for your time, of course."

"Thank you for the offer," Colson said, "but I don't need to be paid for this. I mean, well, I could accept a nice bottle of scotch if you insist, but heck, it'll be exciting to think that I've worked with the police on a murder investigation. And it's good timing, because just last night I finished the mystery I was reading. So now on to the next mystery. And a real one to boot."

"Well, I really appreciate it, Dr. Colson," Saxby said. "I think the bottle of scotch sounds like a great deal for the town. Are you saying you'll be able to start on this soon, then?"

"Sure, I've got some fresh coffee," Colson said. "I'll spread it out on the table and start looking at it right away. It'll take some time, but I'll put my thoughts on it together for you as soon as possible."

"That's just great, then," Saxby said. "I appreciate it. One of my officers, Sergeant Barstow, spent some time trying to organize it. Not everything is dated, but she did what she could to put it in some semblance of order. I hope that helps rather than hampers you."

They were interrupted just then when a strange electronic melody filled the room. Colson reached over to the counter to pick up his phone, tapping a few times to stop the sound and read a message that had popped up. "Sorry about that. I had set an alarm to remind me about something I was thinking of doing tonight, but I think I'll dig into your project instead."

"Oh, I hope I'm not making you miss out on something important."

"It's fine, really," Colson said. "There's a conference going on in Atlantic City this week, and an old friend of mine is one of the presenters tonight. He's hosting a discussion on emerging technologies of solar energy. I've been to his talks and worked with him in the past, and I don't need to catch every appearance. We had talked about dinner tonight but—wait a minute. Wait one minute here, Chief Saxby. Something just occurred to me. You told me a few minutes ago that you met with Brewster Atwater right before you came to see me, correct?"

"That's right," Saxby said. "We talked for twenty minutes or so at his office in town. Mark Allen suggested him as someone who might have a feel for … how can I put it … ah, the *temperature* of the people who would likely be against a wind farm."

"I've crossed paths with Atwater, and people like him, two or three times in the past," Colson said, "but not for some years. A cagey character as I recall. May I ask how your meeting with him went?"

"Hmmm. I can see how you might describe him as cagey," Saxby said, "though I can't say I had the sense that he was hiding anything, unless he really pulled one over on me. That doesn't happen often, but it has happened. To put our meeting in a nutshell, it was basically, sure, lots of people would be negatively affected by construction of a wind farm, but not to the level of wanting to use violence against anyone. He said, 'We aren't thugs' at one point."

"That sounds like him, far as I know," Colson said. "Anyway, the reason I bring that up is that I know you're interested in talking to some players who would have an interest in stopping the wind farm."

"Yes, but not just that," Saxby said. "I'm interested in both sides. People who want to stop it and people who support it. That's because, frankly, we don't know yet why Forbes was attacked. I was hoping you could help with that, with all of this stuff in the box."

"I understand," Colson said. "Which is why my suggestion to you is that you should talk to my friend up at that conference in Atlantic City. His name's Gerry Harmon, and I can't think of anyone who would know better than him who you should look at aside from Atwater. He's been across the table from all the power players. You know, the ones who are always fighting the latest solar idea, wind power idea, you name it. Gerry was with ExxonMobil for years before he did a one-eighty and started consulting for Greenpeace. He was with them for at least a few years. Nobody knows both sides better than him."

"That doesn't sound like a half-bad idea," Saxby said. "I'll give it some thought."

"Of course, but don't think about it for too long," Colson said. "His presentation is tonight. Here, let me check the email." He took a minute to scroll through his phone before reading a few lines. "Here it is. The conference is at Harrah's, and Gerry is doing his presentation tonight at seven. Knowing him, I'm sure it'll be interesting, but you could time things to meet up with him just after. Think about it, and if you decide to go up there, I'll call him and pave the way, but I'm sure he'll be glad to help."

"I'll do that, thanks," Saxby said. "I'm taking the idea very seriously. My fiancée might like the excuse to get away for the night. I'll get back to you on that within an hour or two."

After checking in with Doreen at the station, Saxby took a thirty-minute mental break by doing a routine patrol through the town. While he kept a careful eye out for anything of concern as he cruised the streets, the normalcy of the basic patrol gave him a bit of a mental refresh. Though it was only late afternoon, he felt like it had already been a full day of meeting with people. The few minutes of quiet time while rolling around town in the car allowed him to take a small step back and focus on next steps in the Forbes case.

He wanted to meet with Windsor Bell, preferably together with Sergeant Barstow. Dr. Bell was the scientist who had apparently bent Barstow's ear earlier, talking about her concerns that some unknown entity might be threatening their work at the lab. He was interested to hear for himself what she had to say if allowed to ramble on. Another priority was getting in to see Dr. Arthur Hill, the scientist who had worked most closely with Forbes. Saxby considered it a possibility that the time to declare Hill an actual suspect in the attack was drawing near. *But how can I do that? There's no damn evidence! I need at least something before I bring him in.* Saxby knew very well that a trail can grow cold fast, and they needed to catch a break soon. *This guy Gerry Harmon might be part of that break, so, Atlantic City it is.* He pulled over to park while he made a series of calls.

The first one was to Clemson Colson, who told Saxby he'd give Harmon a call and get right back to him, which he did about five minutes later. The result was that Saxby would look for Harmon at one of the bars off the gaming floor at Harrah's at eight o'clock.

His next call was to his fiancée, Angela Andrews.

"Well, yeah, I don't see why I can't take the night off," Angela said. "There's nothing critical I need to do tonight, as long as we're back fairly early in the morning. Will you at least have some time for us to have cocktails and a nice dinner?"

"Absolutely. We need to go to Harrah's, so if you would handle getting us a room and dinner reservation, that would be a help. No holds barred," Saxby said. "Colson tells me his friend is available to meet with me at eight, so I'll do that after our dinner while you play the slots or shop the shops."

"Wow, you really know how to show a girl a good time, Chief Saxby," Angela said. "I will take care of all that and start throwing a bag together."

His next call, a long one, was to Sergeant Barstow, catching her at her desk. He brought her up to date on the developments of the day so far, and his plans to meet with Gerry Harmon that evening at Harrah's Casino.

"I'm hoping he can give us some hints as far as who we should be looking at," Saxby said. "That is, if this thing really does come down to who's pro or con on the wind farm and what they might be capable of doing about it.

Colson sure seemed to think he's the guy who knows all the players."

"Well, I guess at this point we'll take any hints we can get, right?" Barstow said. "What's your latest thinking on Arthur Hill?"

"You know what, Vic," Saxby said, "we need something on him. Something to work with, and I think we might be getting close. Let's just keep an eye on him for now, until further notice. I don't mean a whole stakeout or anything like that, just cruise by his place every once in a while, see how things look."

"I think I can handle that," Barstow said. "I'll use my own car just in case he's up to anything and keeping his own lookout."

They talked for a few minutes longer, covering odds and ends, including a general department update and anything significant going on in town, before signing off. Saxby started the car and headed home to get ready for an evening in Atlantic City.

11

Gerry Harmon's presentation ran a little long, and it was almost half-past eight when he and Saxby managed to sit down together at a table in one of the quieter parts of the casino, close to the baccarat tables and farther from all the slot machines. They ordered a round of beers and chatted briefly before Saxby—for what he hoped would be the last time for the day—launched into a compact summary of the Forbes case, leaving out many details and not using real names. "Pardon the lack of specifics there," Saxby said, "but this case is early days now and I have to keep a lot of it in confidence. The main point is that it seems like this man's death probably has to do with his work, and I'm getting hints—only hints at the moment—that it could have something to do with whether or not this wind farm gets built and who might stand to benefit from either outcome. On that topic, I'm out of my element and hoping you could help orient me." Harmon listened with great interest, interrupting several times with questions or comments.

"So, frankly," Saxby said, "we're very short on evidence right now—physical or even circumstantial. The wind farm, and how—or if—this scallop research might figure into it. My instinct is telling me it does, but that's about all I have to go on at the moment. Yet. Your friend Clemson Colson is going through the man's personal papers right now, and I'm hoping that'll give us something."

"If there's something there to be found," Harmon said, "Clemson will find it. Even if not, he should at least be able to flesh out the background some more, about this scientist and what he was working on. You plan to meet with that other scientist again also, is that right? The one who worked most closely with the dead man?"

"Yes, I plan to have a chat with that person tomorrow," Saxby said. "See if I can get a feel for his state of mind. We have evidence that tells us there was someone there at the house, but nothing that points specifically to him or any other particular person. With that said, he's the one who worked most closely with the guy, and he fits the general profile. They could've had a fight. Anyway, we're keeping an eye on him. Meanwhile, if this thing turns out to be bigger than it looks, and we need to start taking a serious look at some of the big players in my area, who are they? Colson thought you might be able to help with that. That's why I'm here."

"I think I can probably help you there," Harmon said. "You got off to a really good start by dropping in on Brewster Atwater. He represents a good chunk of the fishing and shellfish industry up and down the coast, particularly from say, around Brigantine and south to Cape May. I've met him a few times, though it's been some years. He's part of a kind of informal syndicate, or maybe more like a cabal, of bigwigs who tend to always be on the 'anti' side of anything to do with wind, or solar, or protecting the environment—that same old story. Because I've spent so much time working with those kinds of projects, or testifying as an expert witness, I've bumped into those characters more than a few times. Here, I had a little free time this afternoon and I made a couple notes for you."

Harmon unzipped a thin leather portfolio and fished out a few items. He handed Saxby a photograph. "An old friend of mine sent me that pic about six months ago. He took it himself at a charity event in Ocean City. That group right there is a good representation of the men I've been talking about. I call them 'the power brokers.' Well, sometimes I call them jerks, but aside from that, I and some other people I've worked with call these guys the power brokers. Except that one man on the left—I don't know who that is."

Saxby looked closely at the picture of five men standing together on a stone patio while other small groups of people scattered in the background appeared to be mingling and chatting, many with cocktail glasses in their hands. Saxby could barely suppress a groan when he realized that he knew the man on the left. "I see Brewster Atwater here, but I don't know the other three closest to him. But the one on the left you said you didn't know, he's a real charmer. That's Barry Vaughn. He's the president of Tanner Construction, based in Cape May. I've had some dealings with him about a year ago. If there's something bad going on, I wouldn't be surprised if he was in on it."

"Tanner Construction you say. Now that is very interesting," Harmon said. "I'm pretty sure that's the company that's planning to build that giant condo complex at the top of North Wildwood. Right there on Hereford Inlet. Wow. I'm making a supposition here, but that might be a perfect example of a company that would just hate to have a slew of wind turbines built off the coast. NIMBYs, you know—not in my back yard. They don't want all that going on right offshore—they want to sell condos, and they think something like that ruins the view. Like I said, I'm just guessing, but you know, if the shoe fits. And he fits right in with the others."

"It does seem that way, doesn't it?" Saxby said. "So that's Barry Vaughn, and there's Atwater. Do you know who these other three are?"

"Yes, from left to right," Harmon said, tapping a finger on the picture, "that's Rand Pearson. He's the owner of one of the biggest scallop operations in Cape May County. He's part of Garden State Shellfish along with Atwater. Next is Jed Gatling, owner of Gatling Pipeline, which is one of the biggest refinery supply and maintenance companies on the east coast. He also owns Gatling Refinery in Bayonne, which is currently leased to ExxonMobil. He likes to play up the idea that he's a descendent of Richard Gatling—you know, the guy who invented the Gatling gun—the first successful machine gun. Who knows, maybe it's true. This last man here, that's Bruce Devere. He's president of DelVal United, which, like Gatling Pipeline, is another of the biggest refinery construction, maintenance, and supply companies in New Jersey and up through the Northeast."

"Okay, so these four, plus maybe now adding Barry Vaughn," Saxby said, "are the folks you and your friends like to call the 'power brokers.' You think they're some of the most likely people to be mixed up in trying to stop a wind farm?"

"Yes, Chief Saxby, I do," Harmon said. "Look, I can't sit here and actually accuse them of crimes, but if the case you're working on turns out to involve these kinds of big power players, I'll tell you, if one or more of these guys doesn't have their hands in it, I'm Marilyn Monroe. These guys are pure as the driven slush."

"Well, you sure don't look anything like Marilyn Monroe," Saxby said. "Can I hang on to this picture?"

"Yes, that's a copy I made for you," Harmon said. "And take the list too. I've made a few notes for each of them. You can add your own on Barry Vaughn if you think that makes sense. We know why someone like him might have an interest in stopping a wind farm—that's all about big wind turbines ruining the view from an expensive condo balcony. The oil men, like Gatling and Devere, just don't want to see renewable energy in general getting any traction. At least they want to hold it off for as long as they can, you know, so they can keep raking in big bucks from the oil and refinery business. The New Jersey economy has a major refinery sector. They want a wind farm in their back yard like I want a rusty nail stuck through my foot."

"Yeah, I see what you mean. They see the future coming up fast and they don't like it," Saxby said. "Hey, I know it's getting late, but there's one other thing I wanted to ask you about. I've told you how, with this scallop Alzheimer's research, we don't know yet whether that was going to be successful or not. In the interest of fairness to these power brokers, do you know anything about the other side of the project? Like the wind farm company. Have you had dealings with them?"

"I have not yet had the pleasure," Harmon said, as he added notes to the power broker list, "but I can tell you a little bit about the company that's hoping to build the farm off Cape May County. Trans-Oceanic Wind is their name, and the CEO is a lady by the name of Claudine Bouchet. She's a French national who I think inherited the reins from her father years ago. I've never met her, but I've heard that she's tough. If I'm on the right track at all about these power brokers, and they were going up against her, I'd bet there could be some sparks flying."

"Well, you've given me some good information and a lot to think about," Saxby said, after they had talked for a while longer. "I really appreciate your time. I'll let you know how the case shakes out. Next time you find yourself in Cape May I hope you'll let me take you out for dinner, or drinks, or both."

"Both sounds good," Harmon said. "I'll make a note to take you up on that. And yes, please let me know how it turns out. You've got a fascinating case here, and I like to know when I'm right or wrong."

At that, he went off in the direction of the nearest bank of elevators. Saxby settled up with the cocktail waitress before going off himself in search of a few stolen moments of good R & R with his fiancée, and after that, a good night's sleep.

12

By seven-thirty the next morning, Saxby and Angela were well into a luxurious room-service breakfast in their suite at Harrah's Casino Hotel. They had already agreed that Angela's ambient sound machine, with the gentle sound of waves crashing against the shore, had been a great help to both of them in getting a surprisingly restful sleep.

"I know we have to get going soon," Angela said, "but I'm gonna miss that Jacuzzi. That's a nice one. It's been too long since I've had champagne in a giant bathtub."

"Well now, I hope you aren't already forgetting that we have a pretty nice Jacuzzi in our bedroom at home," Saxby said, as he refilled their coffee cups before helping himself to some more fresh mango and papaya. "We usually have champagne in the fridge too."

"No, I'm not forgetting anything about our wonderful house, Tate my dear," Angela said. "It's just a special treat to be in a fancy hotel room. Let's remember to do this every once in a while, you know, like a mini-vacation."

"I'm all for it," Saxby said, "let's do it. Not right in the middle of a murder investigation would be best, though I think coming up here to meet with Harmon was time well spent. He gave me some really good information that might help with the case."

"Where do you think it's going next?" Angela said. "With your case? The case of the murdered scientist?"

"I'm really hoping to hear from Clemson Colson today," Saxby said. "The guy you heard on Mark's radio show. If he could tell us something about what Forbes was thinking lately, or worried or upset about, that might shake something loose. I've got to spend some time looking into these people today. I need to learn whatever I can about them."

"What are you thinking about Barry Vaughn maybe being part of that group?" Angela said. "Those power people."

"The 'power brokers' is what Harmon was calling them," Saxby said. "Yeah, I'm surprised to see him pop up in the picture, mostly because I've tried hard to not think about him. I'm less surprised to think that he might be mixed up in some crazy illegal scheme. I think that's probably right up his alley. To be fair to him though—and to Atwater and the others—this is all just one angle to look at. They might have nothing at all to do with Lewis Forbes."

"Now that it's been more than a year," Angela said, "and you've got some distance from it, do you still think he might have gotten away with murder?"

"You know, a minute ago I said how I've tried not to think about him," Saxby said, "but actually he does cross my mind once in a while. I doubt he ever pulled a trigger or stuck in a knife, but my gut tells me he had to be involved. Pulling the strings somehow, is my guess. Convincing other people to do the dirty work. But I can't prove it, and anyway the county says the case is closed. They like things closed up nice and neat. Especially back then in an election year."

"Not that I disagree with you," Angela said, "but try not to get too cynical. Remember, you're one of the good guys."

Saxby laughed at that. "Thanks, Ang, I'll keep that in mind. So, how about we good guys get it together and head back on down to the southern tip. There's lots of work to do and crooks to catch, you know."

When Saxby got into the police station just after ten, the first thing he did was take a thirty-minute tour around the office, taking a few minutes to check in and talk with every officer he could find. He asked them each about how they were doing, what they were working on, and did they have any concerns he could help with. For years it had been his habit to try to do this daily when time allowed, or at least several times a week. He felt strongly that it helped with morale and a general feeling of camaraderie. He had noticed Sergeant Barstow waving from her desk as he made his way through the room, and saved her for last, sitting down in her guest chair.

"Good morning to you too, Vic. Please tell me you have news of some exciting development."

"Actually, I think I might," Barstow said. "And good morning to you too, by the way."

"Well, lay it on me, then," Saxby said. "I could use a little good news. After that, I'll tell you about my meeting up in AC."

"Okay, sounds like a good deal," Barstow said. "So, you gave that box of papers and other junk from Forbes' place to this Colson guy to see if he could sort it out and translate some of it for us, right? Before that, I made copies of about the last six months of his appointment planner."

"Right, I remember you told me that," Saxby said. "That must have taken hours."

"A couple, but it wasn't that hard," Barstow said. "There were a lot of blank days, including almost all of the weekends. One thing is, he noted down his phone calls as if they were meetings, or at least the work-related ones. I don't do that. Do you do that, Chief?"

"Hmmm, not usually, unless there's some special reason to," Saxby said. "Did you find lots of calls?"

"Not a whole lot, no," Barstow said. "I was able to find at least a little bit of info on all of them. He had occasional calls with other scientists in his field or related, including one to a lab up in Woods Hole, and looks like three calls to another marine research lab in Greenport, New York. That's up on the north fork of Long Island. Several calls to some fishery in New London. Of course I'll be calling those people, but I found something else that I think is more interesting."

She paused long enough for Saxby to raise an eyebrow and make a 'don't leave me hanging' hand gesture.

"Going back about ten weeks, up to a week before he died, he noted five calls with a person by the name of Diana Rubens, who has a 202 area code."

"Interesting, Washington D.C.," Saxby said. "Is this person another scientist?"

"Nope. Turns out she's a senior aide to Senator Charles Thackery, of Maryland."

"I think this is the part where I say, 'The plot thickens,'" Saxby said.

"Yep, that's the first thing I said to myself too," Barstow said. "I played some phone tag this morning with this person, Diana Rubens, and finally managed to get her on the phone. She was in a big rush and we only talked for about a minute. Turns out she knows Cape May and used to visit with her parents when she was a kid. Anyway, I told her who I was and that I was looking for some background information relative to a homicide case we're working on. She said she was expecting to get a break soon and would call me back when she could talk." Barstow looked at her watch. "Going by what she said, she could call any minute."

"I'm guessing you probably didn't have any chance to ask her what the calls with Forbes were about," Saxby said.

"That's right, not yet," Barstow said. "She seemed very polite and respectful, but also was rushing me off the phone. That's why I'm keeping an ear out for her call. Meanwhile, do you want to tell me about your adventure in Atlantic City last night?"

Saxby spent fifteen minutes relating the main points of his talk with Gerry Harmon in the cocktail bar at Harrah's. He showed her the notes Harmon had given him along with the photo of the group of powerful men that appeared to now include Barry Vaughn.

"I'm liking all this as a possibility, but that's all it is right now. We have no basis to call any of these people suspects yet."

"Got it, Chief," Barstow said. "But we are leaning in that direction with Arthur Hill, right? Shouldn't we try to have another talk with him tonight?"

"Yeah, he's our best lead at the moment," Saxby said. "Seems to be the person closest to Forbes that we've found. But I was really hoping we'd get something from Clemson Colson before we talk to him. I'd like to have something to go in with. Something worth confronting him with. Where does Hill live?"

"Grant Street, a block in from the beach," Barstow said. "I sat down the block from his place for about an hour last night. He had a lady visitor for most of that time."

"A friend maybe? Something romantic?" Saxby said.

"I ran her plate and looked up what I could," Barstow said. "Looks like his ex-wife from a few years back. So probably not romantic, but stranger things have happened. They don't have kids, but maybe they just stay in touch for old times' sake. After she left, he went out to a detached garage at the back of the driveway and was out there for a long time. It has an upstairs, like maybe an in-law apartment or something like that. I cruised by twice before I clocked out, and the lights were still on."

"He must have a work area out there, like a lab or office, similar to what Forbes had," Saxby said. "That must be a thing with these scientists. A place to work at home."

"That's my guess also," Barstow said. "So, anything else to report from last night?"

"The only other thing," Saxby said, "I asked him if he knew anything about the company that's hoping to build the wind farm. He didn't have much on that, except that it's a Europe-based company called Trans-Oceanic Wind, and the CEO is a French lady by the name of Claudine Bouchet. Harmon thought the company was something of a family dynasty situation. So, I'll be spending some time boning up on that along with these other power broker people. That's about it for last night. Oh, I almost forgot— Angela won almost two hundred bucks on the slots."

"Probably not enough to cover the room though, right?" Barstow said.

"More like the room service breakfast," Saxby said, after a laugh. "Well, I'd better get back to my office…"

He was interrupted by the mild buzzing of Barstow's cell phone vibrating on her desk. She grabbed it and looked at the screen. "Washington area code—it's her! How about the conference room?" She took her phone and rushed across to the conference room with Saxby in tow. He shut the door behind them as she hit the button to answer, putting the call on speaker. Barstow set the phone on the table as they both took seats.

"Yes, hello. This is Sergeant Barstow. Is this Diana Rubens?"

"Yes, this is Diana. I'm sorry I couldn't talk earlier, Sergeant, but I was just rushing into a meeting. How can I help you?"

"First, Ms. Rubens, I want to let you know that I've got you on speaker now," Barstow said, "and Chief Saxby is here in the room with me."

"Hello, Ms. Rubens," Saxby said. "This is Tate Saxby, I'm the police chief of Cape May, New Jersey. I know you spoke earlier with Sergeant Vicki Barstow. We appreciate your calling back and will try not to take up much of your time. Are you in your office?"

"Actually no, I'm at the senator's family estate, Morningwood, right now. On Maryland's eastern shore. He's going into a call with the White House chief of staff soon, so I have about fifteen minutes to talk. I'm in an office here by myself at the moment. Is this about the senator?"

"No, I don't think so," Saxby said. "We're just looking for background for a case we're working on. A scientist was killed in town a few days ago in circumstances that appear to indicate foul play. We're in the early stages, so please understand that I can't talk much about the case. Our victim, Dr. Lewis Forbes, worked at a marine research lab here in town, and in the course of trying to find out anything we can about him and what he was working on, Sergeant Barstow came across a number of references to calls with you in his appointment book. We're hoping you can tell us anything you can about Dr. Forbes and why he would have been in touch with your office."

"Wow, I'm in shock," Rubens said. "I mean, my God, how terrible. I really hardly knew him, but he seemed like such a nice man. Why would somebody kill him?"

"We don't have the answer to that yet," Barstow said, "but it's our job to find out, and we're working on it. Can you tell us what your business with him was?"

"Well, I guess so," Rubens said. "I don't see why I can't tell you. Maybe it's my turn to give you a little background. Are you familiar with Senator Thackery?"

"Only what I might have heard in the news," Saxby said. "Please go ahead and fill us in."

"Okay, well, among many other responsibilities,"

Rubens said, "the senator chairs an ad hoc committee that's tasked with disbursing certain available monies targeted to supporting renewable energy research and development. One of many projects on the table is a plan to build a large wind farm off the coast of New Jersey. Southern part—I know you're from Cape May. Offshore in that area."

"Would that be the project that Trans-Oceanic Wind was hoping to do?" Saxby said.

"Yes, that's right. Trans-Oceanic Wind," Rubens said. "A French company I think, but that's about all I can say without digging out the file. So, set that aside for the moment. Now, Senator Thackery's wife, Micheline, died about a year ago after a long struggle with early-onset Alzheimer's disease. She was only in her fifties, and the senator was devasted. Since then, he's become known as a major supporter of funding for Alzheimer's research and everything related to that. Earlier this year, he read something about the research being done at this lab in Cape May, and there were a few brief quotes from one of the researchers—Dr. Forbes."

"I think I see where this is going," Saxby said. "The senator learned about the research being done into the possibility of some extract from our local scallops being used to help treat Alzheimer's, and that piqued his interest. I'm guessing that's when he asked you to get in touch with Forbes."

"Exactly, Chief Saxby," Rubens said. "We had several calls, and established a bit of a rapport. The gist of it was that he was feeling better and better about this or that test and was hoping for a positive outcome. As for details, well, I didn't understand a lot of what he talked about, but I got that he was excited—you know, in his dry, scientist kind of way. We were considering inviting him to testify before one of the senator's other committees, but we never got as far as scheduling anything. Now, well, I guess we never will."

"In the times you spoke with him," Barstow said, "did he ever give you the impression that he felt threatened relative to the research, or intimidated in any way? Anything about clashes with anyone he worked with? Anything could help."

"No, I don't remember getting anything like that from him," Rubens said. "Looking back on it now, my sense is just that he felt good about where things were going, and was open to meeting the senator and sharing what he hoped would be good news."

"There's an angle to all this that we've been learning about this week," Saxby said. "And that is the potential medical value of scallops versus offshore wind turbines. My understanding is that scallop harvesting in a given area would be greatly hampered—or stopped completely—by construction of a wind farm. Was the senator or his team aware of that?"

"Absolutely. People on our team have done extensive research on that, and yes, there's a challenge there," Rubens said. "The senator was very sensitive to it, because he is a strong supporter of Alzheimer's research, and generally so in terms of wind power."

"I'm watching the clock, and I know you don't have much time left," Saxby said, "but I'm going to ask you a hypothetical but pointed question. You're not under oath and I'm just looking for the best gut-level opinion you can give me. If this scallop research were to reach a point where it was clear that there could be significant benefit to treatment of Alzheimer's or other disease, do you think the senator would support this wind farm project?"

"Okay, well, yes, that is a pointed question, isn't it?" Rubens said, after a pause. "Given that I'm not Senator Thackery, but I have worked with him for years, my best guess is that if the scallop research had serious, proven potential, I have no doubt that he would do whatever he could to stop the Trans-Oceanic Wind project. Dead in the water, so to speak."

13

"Well, that sure puts an interesting spin on the whole idea of people trying to stop the research," Saxby said, after the call with Diana Rubens ended. "Like Windsor Bell was telling you."

"Right. Dr. Bell," Barstow said. "She was pretty sure some shadowy 'bad guys' were out there trying to sabotage what they were doing. I'll start digging into Trans-Oceanic Wind and see what I can find out about them. It's hard to wrap my head around the idea that some big company could be behind this, but I guess where there's big money involved, all bets are off."

"Sorry to say it, Vic, but you're right," Saxby said. "There's big money on the table here, and big money can make people do almost anything. We got some interesting info today, so what's next? We're hoping to hear from Clemson Colson any time now. I'm holding out hope that he'll have found something that helps connect the dots to Hill. If not, on a different tack, we have these people

Harmon told me about last night—these power brokers. I've already met with Brewster Atwater, and I was planning to dump Barry Vaughn on you. Aside from the fact that I don't relish dealing with him, I just think he'd respond to you better. If your schedule's clear this afternoon, I don't see any reason to delay going over to talk with him. Thoughts?"

"Well, I don't want to talk to him either, but you're the boss," Barstow said, pausing for effect. "Nah, I'm just kidding with you, Chief, I don't mind having a talk with Vaughn. He doesn't bother me that much. I'll try his office in town first, and hopefully he's not up in North Wildwood at the condo project."

"Great. Thanks, Vic," Saxby said. "You just want a conversation with him like I had with Atwater. Not accusing anyone of anything, just looking to get a feel for where people's heads are in terms of for or against a wind farm. It's reasonable to think a company that wants to sell condos at the beach would be tuned in to that kind of thing."

"Got it, just looking around at all angles, trying to get background on a case," Barstow said. "I know what to do. And if he gives me any backtalk, I'll soften him up with a roundhouse kick to the temple."

"That's a good plan, Vic, but only do that in your imagination while you're driving away," Saxby said. "Let's leave the guy in one piece for now."

As Barstow drove across town towards the office of Tanner Construction, she cautioned herself to keep the conversation on a friendly level rather than letting it get confrontational. She remembered in her prior exchanges with Vaughn that he could be a mixture of charming, humorous, sarcastic, and razor sharp. All that with an underlying dose of conniving. Whether he was somehow involved with the suspicious demise of the founder of Tanner Construction less than a year ago was not something they had been able to prove, but Barstow shared Saxby's strong feeling that he must have had a hand in it. Jeff Tanner, who had fired Vaughn in anger, dead in a suspicious accident, followed within days by his son Paul in a confrontation with police, and within weeks Vaughn at the helm of the company, was a bit much to take, but Barstow was matter-of-fact about it. The justice system had run its course in broad daylight and the case was closed. Neatly, it seemed to many.

At least, Barstow reflected, it wasn't like Vaughn was some kind of maniac, killing people indiscriminately. In the privacy of her cruiser, she broke into a smile as she briefly imagined punching him in the face.

Stop that now, Sergeant. You are a professional!

As she pulled up to the corner across from the Tanner Construction office, she paused for a moment as she noticed several men talking in the driveway between a black stretch limousine and one of the Tanner company pickup trucks. She recognized Vaughn but not either of the other two men, who both looked substantially older than him. With a handshake, the two older men got into the limousine and it drove away, leaving Vaughn alone.

Barstow figured that a business meeting had just ended, and it would be a good time to grab Vaughn for a few minutes. She crossed the street and entered the Tanner lot. Vaughn had been walking back towards the building as she pulled in, but stopped and turned when he heard the car.

"Well, I'll be. Is that Sergeant Barstow?" Vaughn said, coming closer as Barstow got out of her car. "How nice to see you."

"Likewise, Mr. Vaughn," Barstow said. "I saw your last meeting ending just as I was pulling up, and I was hoping it would be a good time for you to spare me a few minutes."

"Of course. I have lots to do, and more meetings coming," Vaughn said, "but I can always spare some time for the local police. It's such a nice day. How about right over here in the side yard?" He gestured to a cleared rectangle of lawn off to one side of the main building, where there was a trio of picnic tables with benches. Barstow followed him to the nearest table.

"May I assume that you're here on official business?" Vaughn said.

"Well, I'm working on official business," Barstow said, "but I'm only here to speak unofficially with you."

"That's interesting, Sergeant," Vaughn said. "And at least a little bit circuitous. What can I do to help?"

Among other things Barstow had been thinking during the drive over, she had spent a few minutes on how best to open the conversation with Vaughn, deciding in the end to trust her instincts and wing it. "I'm hoping you can help with a little background, given the type of work Tanner Construction does. We have a homicide case that we're working on. Perhaps you heard about Dr. Lewis Forbes?

He was one of the scientists from the marine research lab out on Poverty Beach."

"Yes, I did hear about that. Just a few days ago, wasn't it?" Vaughn said. "That's really terrible. As far as I know, those folks were just working on finding cures for various diseases."

"That's right, and yes, it is quite a shame," Barstow said. "It appears he died as a result of a violent attack, and it appears further that the motive may have had something to do with the work he was doing and how that could affect plans to build a large wind farm off the coast."

"I heard some snippet a long time ago about an idea to build a wind farm off Cape May County, but I don't know anything about it," Vaughn said. "Those people out at the marine center were working with fish, right? Or maybe it was clams. Their blood or something else from their bodies could be used to treat human diseases. Is that it? I've read that horseshoe crab blood is used for something like that."

"You're on the right track, Mr. Vaughn," Barstow said. "Except that it's mostly scallops they were working on. From what we understand so far, they were looking at the possibility that something from scallops could be used to help treat human diseases."

"I see. Hmmm. I imagine if they had some great break-through," Vaughn said, "the government might step in to protect the scallop beds. That would probably put paid to any plans to build a wind farm. I suppose scallop fisherman might hate it too, but maybe they could work out a way to sort of 'share' the scallop. Anyway, that's not an area I know anything about. Well, other than to say that I like my scallops sauteed with lots of butter and garlic. In any case, aside from that, Tanner Construction doesn't have anything to do with scallops."

"Understood, Mr. Vaughn," Barstow said. "We are aware of the concerns that scallop fisherman might have about a wind farm affecting their ability to harvest scallops, but we're also thinking about other parties who might have a strong position against construction of a wind farm. People heavily invested in the fossil fuel industry for example. Or also..."

"People heavily invested in building and selling condominiums at the seashore," Vaughn said. "Pardon the interruption there. That's why you came to see me, isn't it?"

"I have correctly remembered that you are very sharp, Mr. Vaughn," Barstow said, allowing a smile. "I hope you'll agree that your industry could be seen as an entity that doesn't want to see a lot of giant windmills sticking up out in the ocean."

"Round up all the usual suspects it is, then," Vaughn said, with a laugh. "Really though, Sergeant, your comments are fair and your logic is reasonable. The thing is, times have changed, and we do research on these things. Certainly, there are people who would look out at wind turbines and think it's all terrible or that they ruin the view, and there are other people who would think more like, 'Wow that's cool and the future is here.' Regardless, it's happening, right? If this wind project doesn't go through, others will pop up soon enough. Our industry is mostly *laissez-faire* about it. Hands off and what's going to happen will happen. To answer a question you haven't asked yet—no, I find the idea of anyone resorting to violence to try to stop the wind farm highly unlikely. I just can't see it."

"I was planning to ask you something like that, yes," Barstow said, "and I appreciate your candid answer. If not actual violence, would your opinion extend to something else, like, say, sabotage? Like maybe people doing something to try to slow down this research? I'm asking about construction in general, not simply your company."

"Well, you know I can only really speak for Tanner Construction," Vaughn said, "but I do try to have my ear to the ground as far as what's going on in the industry. Where are the opportunities, what are the threats to business— that kind of thing. My opinion is the same, Sergeant. I just don't see it. Of course, as you know, there could always be some angry nut going off the rails, but I consider even that unlikely."

"Well then," Barstow said, as they both got up from the picnic table, "you've helped me get a general feeling for one possible aspect to our case, and I'm grateful for your time. Which I think I've taken enough of for now."

"You are most welcome, Sergeant. You know, there's something that comes to mind about all this," Vaughn said. "It seems like, if builders wanted to stop the wind farm, they would want this scallop research to succeed. Same for scallop fisherman or for oil and gas people, right? Yet, you're saying someone killed this scientist who was working hard to make it succeed. Very interesting. On the other side of the coin, if you were Trans-Oceanic Wind, you would *not* want the research to succeed. But what is the use of killing one member of a team? That isn't going to stop the research. You do have a puzzle on your hands,

Sergeant. Feel free to call if you have any further questions."

It was late afternoon when Barstow got back into the station, finding it empty, apart from Doreen at the front desk and Saxby back in his office. After downing a power bar at her desk and making a cup of tea in the station kitchen, she knocked on his open door.

"Hey, Vic," Saxby said, closing a file he had been looking through and setting it in his OUT box. "I hope you got through your meeting with Barry Vaughn unscathed. How did it go?"

"Well, you know he's a character, that's for sure," Barstow said. "A real charmer. But really, it was fine. Setting aside whatever we may think of him, he was pleasant and seemed happy to help. Putting on an act maybe, but all in all I think we had a good conversation."

"Well, good, then," Saxby said. "I wouldn't have asked you to go see him if I didn't have every confidence that you could handle him. What was the result?"

Barstow took a few minutes to summarize the Vaughn meeting for Saxby.

"I think the main takeaway is that, from his point of view, condo buyers' or builders' feelings about a wind farm blocking the view wouldn't be enough to drive anyone to violence. Whether or not that's true, it's my read that he was being sincere. Aside from, well, there was one small thing I noticed, that's probably nothing, but..."

"Trust your instinct, Vic," Saxby said. "Let's hear it."

"Okay. I really doubt it's anything, but who knows," Barstow said. "When I first mentioned a plan to build a wind farm off the coast, he said he had heard something about it a while ago but didn't know anything about it. Very vague, which is fine, except that at the end of our conversation he specifically mentioned Trans-Oceanic Wind."

"Hmmm. That's worth filing away," Saxby said. "Though a slip like that almost seems out of character for him. Maybe he's hiding something, or maybe he just remembered the name of the company. Anything else?"

"One other thing. And I think this might be a biggie," Barstow said. "After you saw Brewster Atwater at his office, didn't you tell me that he was very tall, like six-five or something, and looked like an ad for Ralph Lauren?"

"I could have mentioned that, sure," Saxby said, "and that's a fair description of him. Why? Do you think you saw him?"

"Yes, I think I may have," Barstow said. "Before I drove up to Tanner Construction, I sat across the street for a minute while Barry Vaughn talked with two men in the driveway. It looked to me like a meeting had just ended and Vaughn had walked them to their car. They shook hands and the other two got into a Cadillac stretch limo and left. I didn't get a good look at the other guy, but the way the chauffer acted towards him I figure it was his limo. He's one of those other power broker guys you told me about, Jed Gatling. The one who says his great-grandfather invented the Gatling gun."

"Interesting. If you're right, and they were meeting with Barry Vaughn," Saxby said, "then it's really starting to look like Harmon was right and this power broker group is a real thing. The very tall man sounds like Atwater, based on your description, but what makes you think the other man is Jed Gatling?"

"I try to remember my training, Chief," Barstow said. "And I keep my eyes open. The license plate was 'Gat Gun1,' and it's registered to Gatling Pipeline Inc."

14

"Well, bravo to you, Vic. Good work," Saxby said, after a long pause. "Last night, Gerry Harmon tells me about this group of people he calls the power brokers, and the next day you see three of them with their heads together. Amazing." He took a sheet from one of the folders on his desk and read for a few seconds. "That leaves Bruce Devere, representing big oil and gas, and Rand Pearson with his scallop fleet as the two we haven't yet seen or met. I might have to track them down soon. Sure looks like this power broker thing might really be a thing, if you know what I mean."

"Oddly enough, Chief, I do know what you mean, and I second the idea," Barstow said.

At that, they both retreated into their thoughts and the room went quiet for a moment, with Barstow scribbling something on her pad while Saxby leaned back in his chair to stare at the ceiling. Almost a minute had gone by when Saxby's desk phone rang, breaking the silence with its jarring rattle. "It's Colson," he said, before punching the button to answer.

Barstow listened to Saxby's side of the brief conversation before he ended the call. As he stood up and came around the desk, she could tell that the phone conversation had given him a jolt of energy.

"He's finished going through Lewis Forbes' papers and he says he found some interesting things to talk to us about. He's in a rental condo up on the beach. Want to come along and see what's up?"

Barstow was already up and gathering her notes. "I wouldn't miss it for the world, Chief. Seems like we might be making some progress today."

"I'll meet you up front in five minutes," Saxby said. "And I'll drive. I need to stop at Collier's for a bottle of scotch."

"A sixteen-year-old Lagavulin, my word. I didn't expect you to put such a dent in the town's budget just for me, Chief Saxby. I would have been thrilled with some good old Johnny Walker. But thank you nonetheless." Saxby had presented Colson with the bag from the liquor store as soon as he had greeted them at the door and shown them in. Both officers accepted Colson's offer of coffee, and the three of them took seats around the kitchen island, where numerous piles of papers of various sizes and shapes were laid out neatly.

"This was an interesting project," Colson said. "Obviously I never met Lewis Forbes, but I almost feel like I know him now. He was certainly a hard-working and dedicated man of science. Like any good researcher should, he kept lots of notes. He did a lot of that in somewhat of a journal form, but also, he had a habit of grabbing whatever sheet of paper was available and scribbling something down. He must have had various sizes of pads sitting around handy. You can see those several notes there in that lavender color. I have some of those pads at home myself. He had his own chicken-scratch, but I've been reading that stuff for years. So I think you're in luck in that he wrote down a lot of his thoughts."

"I imagine that must be a habit that scientific researchers would train themselves to follow," Saxby said.

"Absolutely," Colson said. "It's an essential habit. In this case, it was helpful to me, and I think it'll be helpful to you. Let me explain my process." With that, he began his informal presentation, pointing several times to one or more of the piles on the table, or referring to a sheet or a crumpled note or a bound journal book.

"The first thing I did was to put as much of this as I could into some semblance of chronological order. I had to make a few guesses, but a lot of it was dated, like most of the printed reports and the couple of news clippings, so that was a help. The entries in his personal journal were almost all dated. The sorting that Sergeant Barstow did was also a help. After that, I started back almost a year ago and began skimming through all of it until I got much closer, like around two months ago. Most of that earlier material seemed routine to me, like excerpts from papers by others in the field for the most part. Journal entries and the odd notes I could fit into that chronology were gener-ally just the boring day-to-day materials appropriate to the work he was doing. There were a few entries that give me the impression that he was happy with the other scientists at the lab. For example, there was a line in one of the entries that said '...good work today with Arthur...,' and another that had something like '...lucky to be working with AH and WB on this...' I gather the 'AH' meant Arthur Hill, and the 'WB' must have been someone else he worked with."

"That must be Windsor Bell," Barstow said. "Dr. Bell is one of the other people he worked with along with Arthur Hill. They were the main three people working on the scallop and Alzheimer's project."

"Okay. Well, in any case, I got the impression that he had good relationships with them," Colson said. "Moving on, then, I see a number of references around two or three months ago to the research going very well. He was feeling positive about it. Then, right at the beginning of September, just over a month ago, he finds something that doesn't make sense to him. Let me read you something. It isn't all legible, but here are some fragments I wrote out." He proceeded to read from a legal-size pad, tapping along the words with a pencil.

September 9 ... last test can't be right ... something ... something ... far too much ... something. Going to have to do ... test over. Whole damn week ... something ... something ... make sense...

"And then there's this:"

.   .   .

Run sequences again ... something ... through twelve ...
something ... Fisher and Gardin .... Something-something ... too
cold ... something ... something ... Isl ... ound...

"Most of that was from a few pages that looked like he must have spilled coffee or something on them. A lot of it was illegible, but clearly, he had come across some information he was trying to puzzle out. Am I giving you too much background with this? I could skip ahead to the meat and potatoes if you'd rather I did that."

"You're doing fine. This is some good stuff," Saxby said. "We really appreciate it, but let me ask you something. All this you've put together for us, like a sticky note here, a journal entry there, a notepad—do you have this all together in some kind of timeline, or summary that you could give us?"

"Yes, I do. Mostly," Colson said. "If I had another hour or two, I could finish up a summary for you. And of course, you'll have all this material back in case it was ever needed as evidence."

"Fantastic. So, as long as we can dig back into the source if we need to," Saxby said, "go ahead and give us the CliffsNotes version. Whatever you think are the key points."

"Sure, glad to. I thought you might prefer that," Colson said. He took a moment to shuffle papers and take a few sips of his coffee. "Okay, then. The CliffsNotes version of the meat and potatoes coming right up. Basically, going back almost a year, Forbes and the others were humming along for a while. The last few months of the year and then into this year. There was some progress here and there but nothing exciting. Mostly just plugging away at whatever their process was to determine if proteins in ocean scallops could be used to somehow synthesize a treatment for Alzheimer's disease. Now, obviously I didn't work with them, so there's a lot I don't know, but roughly speaking, things were moving along, if slowly. Then comes whatever it was that he found, like tests that were way out of line or something like that. Looks like he repeated some tests several times, and started to bring more of his work home. During that time, he places a very strange order—I found the actual shipping slip. Here, I made a copy for you. He places an order with a marine research supply company in New London for five pounds of scallops, frozen in the shell."

"Okay, wait a sec please, Dr. Colson," said Barstow. "Forbes is a scientist doing all kinds of research on scallops. Why is it strange that he placed an order for scallops?"

"Very good, Sergeant," Colson said. "The thing is, it isn't strange that he placed an order for scallops. What's strange is that he placed an order for *five pounds* of scallops, and from New London, Connecticut. Now, I called the supplier and spoke with a very helpful lady, and I hope it's okay that I told her I was working with the Cape May police on a homicide investigation. I swore her to secrecy."

"That's fine," Saxby said, with a laugh. "No doubt she was excited to help. What did she tell you?"

"She confirmed my suspicion that five pounds is an oddly small amount, given that the standard supply shipment would be a forty-pound sack. Also, the scallops that were ordered were local to just south of New London. That's what Forbes had asked for specifically. Now, here's the kicker. He paid for the order with his personal credit card, and he had them shipped to his home."

"Let's make a note to check with Three and Brody to see if they found any scallops when they searched his place," Saxby said, looking at Barstow. "So, he's working on scallops for a year or however long, then suddenly sees something that startles him. You said you thought it was around then that he started to be more withdrawn. It's also then that he decides he needs a sample of scallops from the New London Area, which would be the eastern part of Long Island Sound. What the heck does all this mean?"

"And he has them shipped to his house," Barstow said. "Like he didn't want the other people at the lab to know about it, but why not?"

"Wait a sec, I might have it. I'm just picturing New London," Saxby said, "which is on the Connecticut coast, roughly across the sound from the north fork of Long Island. Can you read that second quote again—with all the something and something stuff?"

"Sure, it's right here," Colson said. He picked up the paper and read aloud:

Run sequences again ... something ... through twelve ... something ... Fisher and Gardin ... something ... something ... too cold ... something ... something ... Isl ... ound ... control...

.   .   .

"That's it. I get it now," Saxby said. "That very last part is a reference to Long Island Sound, which is the body of water between Long Island and the Connecticut coast. And the 'Fisher' and 'Gardin' fragments must be referring to Fishers Island and Gardiners Island, which are two of the islands in the sound between New London and Montauk Point."

"Of course that's it. That has to be it," Colson said. "He found something that suddenly made him want to focus on that area, but what?"

"Here's the copy of the receipt you made for us," Barstow said, holding up the sheet. "And I see from these markings that the original must have been folded up. Is the actual slip right here?"

"Sure, it's in one of these piles," Colson said. He leafed through one of the stacks of papers for a few seconds before pulling out a crumpled sheet and handing it to Barstow.

"A lot of times when I buy something and get a paper receipt," Barstow said, "I'll fold up the receipt so it's easier to put away, but I'll write a note on the back, like 'new tires' or 'gift for mom' or whatever. And here, look, bingo. There's a little scribble on the back, right over the crease. 'Court' or 'can't' or something like that."

"Let me see that," Colson said. "I just spent a day deciphering his writing." Barstow handed over the paper. "Court maybe—no. It's 'control.' That's what it says. He got his scallop shipment and wrote a note on the receipt, like you do. He ordered these scallops as a control sample."

"Is it possible that he saw something in the scallops he was working with at the lab that made him suspect they had been brought in from Long Island Sound?" Saxby said. "And he ordered those scallops from New London as a control sample, like to rule something out, or confirm something he suspected? Does that make sense?"

"I think you might make a good scientist, Chief," Colson said. "Yes, that makes sense. That would fit with what we have here. With the specific expertise that Forbes had, I have no doubt that he might have been able to tell if a given shellfish had been harvested from one body of water versus another. Animals can be very affected by their environment. It might not be a good comparison, but flamingo feathers, for example, are bright pink largely because of all the brine shrimp they eat. It's reasonable to think shellfish could carry some sort of unique environmental marker."

"Just going along with this idea for a minute," Saxby said, "can I assume that you didn't find any indication of who he suspected might have done this? Swap scallops, I guess, if that's what we're talking about."

"No, nothing like that I'm afraid," Colson said. "I looked for it but didn't find it. It occurred to me that he probably decided to play it close to the chest and mostly just went quiet."

"Until maybe he finally confronted someone and it all blew up," Barstow said. She and Saxby exchanged looks.

"Not a crazy idea, Vic," Saxby said. "Or someone else found out he knew something and confronted him about it. Anything else in the CliffsNotes?"

"The only other thing is a journal entry from late Tuesday of last week," Colson said. "I thought it looked like a routine scheduling note when I first saw it, but after all this we've just been discussing, it might take on a larger meaning. At the end of his daily entry, he adds 'Need to discuss test panel with Arthur,' with not one but three exclamation points after it. You know, maybe that's your indication of who he suspected."

"That could mean he had stewed on it for a while," Saxby said, "and had finally decided to confront Hill with what he'd found out. Whether that's it or not, it's time we brought Dr. Hill into the station for a talk. Let's plan on picking him up from his home tonight, Vic."

"I'll finish up that summary report for you within a few hours," Colson said. "I can email it to you. If you could leave all these papers with me until then, I'll add a few notes and you can have it all back later or tomorrow."

"If you can get that summary to me within a few hours," Saxby said, "we'll wait to give that a read before dealing with Hill. Cape May and I are in your debt, Dr. Colson. This has been very helpful and worth a lot more than a bottle of scotch. Thanks so much. I'll watch for your email."

"This day is moving along at a good clip, isn't it?" Saxby said as he and Barstow walked to the car. "And I've got a strong feeling it's going to be a late night too."

15

It was just past eight-thirty in the evening when Saxby finished reading the final report Clemson Colson had emailed over. He was thinking about tackling a few items in his IN bin when Barstow and Connor appeared in his office doorway.

"Ah, saved by the bell," Saxby said. "I just finished Colson's report. Have you both been able to read it?"

"Just finished it a minute ago," Barstow said. They both took seats in Saxby's guest chairs. "My take is that it's pretty much what we talked about at his place but in a nice, neat package."

"That's how it looked to me too," Saxby said. "Now, Three, I know you've been caught up in some other projects over the past few days. Do you feel like you're up to speed at this point? Has Vic been taking care of you with the updates?"

"I think so, Chief," Connor said. "I just read the report from Dr. Colson also. You thinking it's time to bring in this Dr. Hill for questioning tonight?"

"Yes. It's time to bring him in and let him feel a little heat," Saxby said. "If there's nothing to it, we'll find out soon enough. I want the three of us to go over in separate cars."

"His ex-wife was there with him last night," Barstow said, "so, I guess it's possible we'll run into her. Not that it should matter—just saying he could have company."

They were interrupted when Doreen poked her head in. "Chief, that address you gave me for Dr. Arthur Hill, wasn't that 650 Grant Street?"

"That's his address, yes," Barstow said. "I went by last night. It's 650 Grant."

"That's what I have too," Saxby said. "What's up, Doreen?"

"Well, I just heard something on the scanner that caught my ear," Doreen said. "That house—650 Grant is on fire."

"We need to get over there on the double," Saxby said, "but first, Vic, get Windsor Bell on the phone and make sure she's okay. Tell her something vague, like, we think Dr. Hill might be in danger and wanted to make sure that she wasn't also. See if she can have a friend or neighbor come over to be with her tonight. I'd rather she not be alone until we know what's going on. Also, contact Brody to have someone outside her place until further notice. After that, come join us over on Grant Street."

As Saxby and Connor pulled up to the house on Grant Street after a short race across town, they could see all the activity was around the detached building at the rear of the driveway. There were two fire trucks already there, along with the fire chief's truck and several private cars that Saxby assumed would have brought other emergency workers to the scene. A small crowd of bystanders had gathered in the street and on the sidewalk. Saxby and Connor were greeted by Officer Megan Hayward as they got out of their cars.

"Looks like it was limited to the garage, and they were able to put it out pretty fast, Chief," Hayward said, "but I think there may have been fatalities. The fire chief's right back there."

"Okay, thanks, Megan," Saxby said. "Stay out here and keep an eye out for neighbors and other gawkers. Let's keep everybody back to the other side of the street. Sergeant Barstow should be here any minute. Oh, and that car there, the old Buick, that might be in the way. If it goes with any of these people standing around, get them to move it, please." He started down the driveway to find the fire chief. It was clear that the fire crew had acted quickly and that the flames were out, but smoke was still coming from the open door, as well as through two windows in the upstairs where the glass had been broken out. Saxby found Fire Chief Barney Goode near the end of the driveway, decked out in his full fire-fighting gear.

"Hey, Barney, looks like your guys have things under control here, that right?" Saxby said.

"Evening, Tate," Goode said. "A pleasure as always. Yeah, pretty much. It was a small fire, and I can tell you right now it was arson, and that's not all, we got two bodies inside, extra crispy with a side order of kerosene."

"Oh shit, Barney," Saxby said. "Dammit. Kerosene, huh? Yeah, I can smell it from out here."

"Vince is just coming out now. Let me grab him and see what he knows," Goode said. He yelled over to another firefighter who had just come out of the building, gesturing to the man to join them. "Hey, Vince, fill Chief Saxby in on what you're seeing in there if you would please."

"Hey, Vince," Saxby said, "I know you've got your hands full here, but any quick summary you could give me could be a help."

"Sure, Chief, no problem," Vince said. "Well, the fire's out now, but it's still kinda hot and smoky in there. Two bodies on the floor maybe fifteen feet apart. They must have died fast, but I guess the ME will have more on that. I can tell you that both of them are adult males. Only one of them still has a recognizable face. The other one is too badly charred, and I think he's wearing a coat, like a leather bomber jacket maybe. I'm guessing the one was the home-owner, and the guy with the coat was a visitor. How it looks to me anyway. There's one car in there but it wasn't affected much by the fire. Most of the space looks kinda like an office or man cave or something like that. There's some broken glass around on the floor, which could be from anything, but for my two cents, it was probably the source of the accelerant."

"Okay, Vince, thanks for that," Saxby said. He turned to nod at Barstow, who had just come down the driveway to join the group. "Did you get Bell?"

"Got her, and she's fine," Barstow said. "Turns out a

friend is staying with her for a few days, so she won't be alone, and we've got a car outside her place."

"Good, that's a relief," Saxby said, before turning back to the firefighters. "Listen, the homeowner was Dr. Arthur Hill, and Sergeant Barstow here met with him recently. Could you take her in there to get a look at the one with the face so we can see if he's our guy?"

"Sure, I can do that," Vince said, after getting a nod from Goode. "I mean, I hope she didn't just eat dinner or anything."

"Thanks for the warning, Vince," Barstow said. "Really, but I think I can handle it. Let's go see if it's him."

"So, kerosene, then," Saxby said, as he and Goode waited for the others to return. "Any thoughts on how it might have gone down?"

"Well, it's way damn too early to say much," Goode said. "But I have to agree with Vince that the one guy lives here and the other one came by to visit. Or came by to burn the place. Hard to say yet, but one thing I know is that arson is a dangerous business. It's totally common for someone who's trying to burn something down to set their own damn selves on fire."

"Makes perfect sense to me," Saxby said. "Just like it's very common for people to cut their hand when they try to stab somebody."

"Yeah, something like that," Goode said. "Anyways, ten'll get you twenty that the guy in the jacket tried to burn the place down and bungled it. You know, burned himself up, lickety-split like. Then there's the broken glass Vince mentioned. Sure, maybe those two guys were enjoying a nice bottle of wine, or a beer, or maybe it was a bottle of kerosene. Anyways, my guys are good at what they do. Give us a little time and we'll figure it out."

"I'm sure you will, Barney," Saxby said. "Do what you gotta do, but I appreciate you giving me your first impressions."

After a few more minutes, Sergeant Barstow returned from her brief tour inside the building. Saxby knew she had a tough hide, but also knew her well enough to see that she was more than a bit affected by what she'd just been shown. She had a small, dark object in her hand, partially wrapped in a piece of rag or towel.

"Yikes, Chief, it's a barbecue in there," Barstow said. "But yeah, that's Hill. I got a picture with my phone. I also got the plate of the car, so we can run it and make sure it's his."

"That was a good idea, Vic," Saxby said. "What else? What's that in your hand?"

"Oh, yeah, this," Barstow said. "The other man in there was more burnt up on the front, but I was able to get a wallet out of his back pocket. It's a little charred, but we've got most of a driver's license."

"Oh, jackpot," Saxby said. "How about taking that to your car right now and see what you can find out. Shouldn't take more than a few minutes."

Barstow nodded and went back up the driveway towards the street, passing Connor on his way back from helping to keep the curious neighbors at bay.

"Chief, a lady just got here who says she's Dr. Hill's ex-wife," Connor said. "She's up there right now with Megan. I told her we believe we have two fatalities but didn't know who they were yet. My take is that she's already decided he's dead. Dr. Hill I mean."

"Alright, that's probably the best thing to tell her right now," Saxby said. "How is she doing? Hysterical or anything like that?"

"No. Upset and some crying," Connor said, "but nowhere near hysterical. She seems like a really strong woman."

"Barney, do you think you can get Vince or one of your other guys to take Deputy Connor here back inside for a quick look around?"

"Sure, Tate, we can handle that," Goode said. "And you don't have to call him Deputy Connor—I know who he is. Three grew up on my street and used to shovel my walk sometimes. Go ahead back there Three and ask for Vince."

"Thanks, Barney," Saxby said. "I guess the widow has arrived, so I'd better go talk to her. Check back with you in a few."

Saxby went back towards the street, where he found Officer Hayward standing with a woman he didn't recognize.

"I'm Chief Tate Saxby of the Cape May police," Saxby said "We haven't met. Are you Dr. Hill's ex-wife?"

"Yes, I am. My name's Gwen. Gwen Hill," she said. "We're divorced about a year now, but I still go by Mrs. Hill. Can you tell me, is he...?"

"Mrs. Hill, all of this has just happened in the last hour or so," Saxby said. "And we've barely just started to investigate, but it does appear that we have two fatalities. I can't say yet if Dr. Hill was one of them. One moment please." Saxby took Officer Hayward aside a few feet and spoke quietly to her. "Megan, go ask Vic if that picture she just took is clean enough to show to Mrs. Hill here. You two can use your judgement. If so, bring it over here right away."

Saxby came back over to Mrs. Hill. "Mrs. Hill, I'm checking to see if we can get a photo that's suitable for you to look at, but I don't know yet, okay? So please bear with me for a few minutes on that. In the meantime, are you okay with taking a few questions?"

Mrs. Hill nodded her assent.

"Did your husband—sorry, Dr. Hill—live here by himself?" Saxby asked.

"Yes, it's just him here in the house," Mrs. Hill said, "since I moved out, maybe two years ago. I come by for dinner sometimes, or just to check in. We like to spend time together. It's just that, well, we became good friends over the years more than anything else. I have a house over on Maryland Avenue that my parents gave me."

"Do you and Dr. Hill have any children?" Saxby said. "Or any other relatives in the area?"

"No, we don't have any children," Mrs. Hill said. "Maybe we've been selfish—I don't know. That just isn't something we wanted for our lives. Other than that, the only one of our parents left is my mother, who's in an assisted living place over in North Cape May. Arthur has a sister and I have two brothers, but nobody anywhere near Cape May. They're all out west."

Barstow and Hayward returned, and Saxby noted that Barstow had her phone in her hand. He threw a question at her with a direct look, and she nodded back.

"Okay, Mrs. Hill," Saxby said, "Sergeant Barstow here

was able to use her phone to take a photo of one of the deceased men inside the building just a few minutes ago. Do you feel comfortable looking at it to tell us if that is Dr. Arthur Hill? Please consider it carefully. This is not required, but it could be helpful to us."

Aside from taking a deep breath, Mrs. Hill didn't hesitate. "Thanks for saying that, but it's fine. Show me the picture. If Arthur's gone, I'd rather know right away."

Barstow tapped the screen on her phone a few times before holding it up for Mrs. Hill to get a close look. Hill looked at the picture for a few seconds before closing her eyes and nodding several times. She put her hands over her face, taking a moment and several deep breaths to compose herself before speaking. When she did, her voice was steady. "Yes, that's him. That's Arthur Hill, my ex-husband. My husband."

"Please accept our condolences, Mrs. Hill," Saxby said. "I know that wasn't easy to do, but it could be helpful. As next-of-kin, you'll need to do that again in an official setting, but that can wait. I think that's probably enough for tonight. I can have one of my officers give you a ride home in your car if you'd like. Do you have a friend or neighbor who can come over tonight to be with you? You know, hang out for a while?"

"You know, that sounds like a great idea," Mrs. Hill said, "because I'd really rather not drive right now. I have a good friend right next door who'll come over, and she always has a bottle of wine handy."

"Okay, great, then. Give us just a few minutes to arrange that," Saxby said. He turned and nodded to Hayward, who then walked away to get on the radio.

"Now, Mrs. Hill, we'd like to talk with you quite a bit more about your husband, but it can wait for morning. Can you come to the station first thing tomorrow?"

They spoke for another minute, firming up an appointment for the next day, before Officer Hayward came back to take Mrs. Hill to her car, leaving Saxby and Barstow alone.

"I know I interrupted you with that," Saxby said, "but were you able to find anything out with the car and the driver's license?"

"Yes, I was just finishing up when Megan found me," Barstow said. "First, the Audi in the garage is registered to Arthur Hill of Cape May, so that's his car. The other body looks like one Jack Rhodes from Port Jefferson, New York, according to his driver's license. He's thirty-six years old, or that's how far he made it anyway. But here's the kicker —that old Buick you pointed out to Megan when you first got here? It's a 2005 LeSabre, which is registered to Jack Rhodes of Port Jefferson, New York."

"Hmmm, interesting," Saxby said. "You seeing what I'm seeing, Vic? There's some connection with Long Island going on here and we need to get to the bottom of it. I asked Three to go back inside for a tour. Let's see if I can get him…"

"Right here, Chief," Connor said, having just walked up behind them. "I just came out. What were you going to ask?"

"We think Vic identified the body that isn't Dr. Hill," Saxby said, "and it looks like his car is right here. I was going to ask you to see if you could find car keys. Don't suppose you found anything?"

"I did check his jacket pockets, but he's pretty well burned up," Connor said. He held up a small wrapped bundle. "There was a kind of lump in the one side that I thought might be keys, but it's mostly all fused together. But here. There's something else he had that I was able to grab. I'm guessing it was stuck in his waistband before the front of his pants mostly burned away."

He opened the cloth to expose the dark metal object he'd taken off the dead man as Saxby and Barstow stepped closer.

"Well, I'll be damned," Saxby said. "I'd say that's an old Colt Detective Special, in .38 caliber. You agree?"

"Yep, I'm sure that's it," Connor said. "I thought it was a Smith and Wesson until I got a closer look, but no, it's a Colt. One shot fired and five still in the cylinder. I guess we're lucky that it didn't get hot enough to cook off the rest."

"One shot fired, then," Saxby said. "We'll need to look for where that bullet went, if he fired it in there."

"I don't think we need to look too far, Chief," Connor said. "Because, right as I was picking this up, the EMT guys were moving Hill onto a stretcher and I guess they saw something and called me over. I'm no doctor, but I'm pretty sure he was shot in the back of the head, and they thought so too."

"Whew. Okay, then. It'll take the doc no time flat to check that when he gets a look at him," Saxby said. "Meanwhile, since we don't have keys, I'm going to get a crowbar from the trunk and open up that Buick. Be sure to bag up that gun and anything else you found, Three."

It took Saxby two minutes to get a large crowbar from

the trunk of his cruiser and take it over to the Buick. "You're sure this is his car, right, Vic?"

"This is it, Chief," Barstow said. "It's a 2005 LeSabre with New York plates, and it's registered to the other body in there. I mean, unless he had the wrong wallet in his pocket."

"I think the odds are in our favor on that one," Saxby said, as he made a powerful but controlled swing at the driver's side window, followed by two smaller swings to clear out more glass around the edges. With most of the window gone, he was able to reach the door lock. Connor came back to join them as Saxby pulled the lever to pop the trunk.

"Well, at a glance, it looks like the usual pile of junk most people have in their trunk," Connor said. He held up a powerful flashlight as Barstow poked around.

"There's the jack, a set of jumper cables," Barstow said, "bunch of rags. Empty water bottles. Pile of old shopping bags—nothing much exciting in here, Chief."

"Hang on, there's a box of something behind the seat here," Saxby said. He lifted a box out from behind the passenger seat and set it on the ground beside the car. Connor pointed the flashlight as he took a small bottle from the box and held it up for the others to see.

"Looks like a half-size wine bottle," Barstow said.

"Yes, I think that's probably exactly what it is," Saxby said. "Except that this one's filled with kerosene and with a rag stuffed in the top. This is a Molotov Cocktail, and there are three more."

"Chief, tell me if I'm wrong," Connor said, "but it seems kinda clear that this guy came here tonight with a plan to kill Dr. Hill and then burn the place down around him. He took one of those inside and must have dropped it after he lit it, or maybe it went up too fast for him to get away."

"I think you probably just summed up what happened fairly well," Saxby said. "We don't know if Hill knew the guy or was expecting him, or if he was invited in or forced his way in, but at some point, he got in, shot Hill, and then lit up one of these. Crude but effective, and he flash-fried himself in the process."

"Well, I think we're about done here for tonight," Saxby said. He put the box back into the car, making sure it wouldn't tip over, and looked at his watch. "If you two would deal with getting this thing towed into the police garage and secured, along with the gun and the wallet, that would be great. After that, go home and get some rest. You know, when I was speaking with Mrs. Hill a little while ago, and I mentioned that we had a lot of questions about her husband, she said something like, 'Yes, and there are some things I want to tell you about him too.' Maybe that's just her way of speaking, or maybe there's something she wants to get off her chest. In any case, I think tomorrow could be another interesting day. Oh, one more thing, Vic, check in with Windsor Bell again on your way out and get her to come into the station tomorrow to talk with us. You can tell her that we believe Dr. Hill has been killed, but that it isn't likely she's in any danger. We're expecting Mrs. Hill at nine, so maybe get Bell in at eleven or twelve. She can tell her boss whatever she wants, but I want her in the station tomorrow. As far as the patrol, I think it's enough to have someone cruise by her place every hour or so for tonight."

"Got it, Chief. I'll call her right now and set it up," Barstow said. "Anything else?"

"No. I think that should do it for now," Saxby said. "I'm going to talk to the fire chief to see if he'll agree to call all of this an accident for a few days. I want to give us a little space on this before everyone in town starts jumping up and down about some kind of murder spree going on."

16

"Thanks for coming in this morning, Mrs. Hill," Saxby said. "And I know the timing is lousy, with everything that happened just last night, but it's critical that we hit the ground running in a situation like this."

"I appreciate that, Chief Saxby," Mrs. Hill said. "But I'll be okay. I had a good cry last night and washed it down with half a bottle of chardonnay, and you know, maybe I can help in some way, even while I'm still numb about it. About 'it'—that's funny. About Arthur."

Mrs. Hill had arrived at the station a few minutes before nine, and was seated across from Saxby and Barstow in the conference room. Saxby had considered meeting in one of the smaller interview rooms, but had decided against it in order not to convey the idea that Mrs. Hill was under suspicion for anything. Barstow had stopped at Starla's café for a box of scones on the way in, and they all had hot cups of coffee in front of them.

"Let me start by giving you a little background," Saxby

said. "We had never heard about Dr. Hill or where he lived or who he worked with until a few days ago. It was this past Monday morning when we learned that a local man here in town had been killed the night before in what looked like a violent attack—an argument that escalated and got out of hand, quite possibly. That man was Dr. Lewis Forbes, who worked with your ex-husband at the Cape Shore Marine Research Center. Did you know Dr. Forbes, by any chance?"

Mrs. Hill looked momentarily stunned, taking a moment before answering. "Dr. Forbes. Lewis Forbes? I ... wow. Ah ... no, I didn't know him, but I was aware he was someone who worked with Arthur. I'd heard the name mentioned a few times, relative to whatever they were working on. You said something about a violent attack. Are you saying that Arthur may have done this? There's just no way. He was a peaceful man."

"I can't sit here and say that your husband—I'm sorry, Dr. Hill..."

"It's okay to refer to him as my husband, Chief Saxby. I know who you're talking about. Please continue."

"Okay, thanks," Saxby said. "We don't know that it was your husband who attacked Lewis Forbes. We don't have any physical evidence to support that, but there is enough circumstantial evidence that we had decided yesterday it was time to bring him in for questioning. We consider it a possibility that your husband went over to Forbes' house to talk to him, or maybe to confront him about something. Things could have gotten heated, and at some point, your husband picked up a heavy object and lashed out with it. I'll repeat that we only see that as a possibility right now.

So, we were about to get in the car last night to go see your husband when we heard about the fire. We got to the scene shortly before you did. Now, I'm not sure exactly what you heard last night, in all the confusion, but there was a second man found inside the building with your husband, also deceased."

"I thought I heard someone say something about 'fatalities'," Mrs. Hill said. "My God, don't tell me it was another of those scientists. Do you know who it was?"

"We're fairly sure he wasn't a local person. Someone from out of town, as a matter of fact," Saxby said. He paused for a few seconds. "What I'm going to say next might be hard to hear, but the thing is, there are strong indications that this second man came here to Cape May with the specific intent to kill your husband, and apparently started the fire in a deliberate attempt to cover up the crime."

"That's just so incredible," Mrs. Hill said. "I mean … I don't really know what to say. Lewis Forbes and now Arthur? What the hell is going on around here?"

"That's what we're trying to answer," Saxby said. "You can help by telling us anything you can think of as far as your husband's recent state of mind or anything that seemed to be bothering him or worrying him. Anything at all that you think might be out of the ordinary for him. Whatever comes to mind could be important."

"I understand. I'm just trying to wrap my head around all of this," Mrs. Hill said. "But I do want to help. I just thought of something that might be nothing, but … you said Lewis Forbes was found Monday morning and that there had been some sort of attack the night before—so,

Sunday night. Do you know about what time that might have been?"

"We think it was probably somewhere between ten and eleven, give or take an hour or so," Saxby said. "Why do you ask that?"

"When I first came in here this morning," Mrs. Hill said, after taking a moment to think something over. "I was in a frame of mind of protecting Arthur. Defending his legacy maybe. Something like that. I'm not exactly sure. But now you're telling me you think someone actually killed him. And now … with this about Lewis Forbes … I just want to help however I can. Help you figure out what happened I guess is what I'm saying. And if Arthur was mixed up in something he shouldn't have been, I'd rather know about it than not."

"We're glad to hear that Mrs. Hill," Saxby said. "We'll be glad to have your help. But tell me, why did you ask about the time of the attack on Lewis Forbes?"

"Yes, well, that was last Sunday night," Mrs. Hill said. "I had been over at my friend Daisy's house on Third Avenue for dinner and to help her with a project she was working on. It went later than I had expected, and I ended up leaving at about ten. It might have been five after, but not much more. So, as I frequently do, I decided to go by the old house. I wouldn't have barged in or banged on the door or anything like that, but if I had seen that Arthur was in his office—you know, the garage—I might have stopped in to say hi. That was something I did every once in a while."

"That must have been about ten or fifteen minutes after ten," Saxby said, "when you drove by. Is that right?"

"Yes, it was right around there, within a few minutes,"

Mrs. Hill said. "But as I came up the road, I saw his car pull out and drive away up to the beach. That's the way I go home from there anyway, so I was behind him for a while. He made the left onto Beach Avenue and I was still behind him. Another car came out of one of the cross streets and got between us, but I could still see him up ahead. We went all the way along the beach until he made a left on Madison. That's where I went straight for a few more blocks until my left onto Reading."

"And you're sure he made that left onto Madison Avenue?" Barstow said. "It couldn't have been another car that got between you along the beachfront?"

"No, I'm sure it was him," Mrs. Hill said. "He had bought that fancy new Audi a few months ago and I found it easy to spot. I must say it occurred to me that it was odd for him to leave the house at that hour. It didn't seem like him, but I didn't think about it all that much at the time. I figured he was running some late errand, like to get milk for breakfast or something like that. He turned down Madison, I went home, and that was that. Looking back on it now, I can't help but wonder if I saw him on his way over to Lewis Forbes' place. Where did he live?"

"Let's just say that, if he turned to go down Madison Avenue," Saxby said, "he could possibly have been on his way to see Forbes, and that is the right timeframe, but let's not get ahead of ourselves. If that really is the direction he was heading, there's still any number of other possible destinations, including the Wawa market. That's good information though. So that was Sunday night. When was the next time you saw him after that, if at all?"

"I saw him the next night, Monday," Mrs. Hill said. "We

had a kind of regular dinner date for most Mondays. I would get Chinese takeout and a bottle of wine and bring it over to the house. We'd have that in front of the TV and then I'd go home not long after dinner. It's so strange, but this is making me look back on everything in a new light. Usually, if I got there before seven, we'd watch *Jeopardy* on channel six. I definitely remember that he was way off his game that night. He just couldn't seem to pay attention to the answers or the categories like he usually did. I remember asking about it and he said something about being distracted by some puzzle or other that he was working on in the lab. I didn't dwell on it because that was a normal thing that could happen on occasion. I was only there for two or three hours, but now that I think about it again, I'd say that something was off that night. Like he was somewhere else. At the time, I just figured he'd had a bad day and I should head home and let him have the rest of the evening to himself, so, that's what I did. That was the last time I saw him."

"You mentioned how these recent developments are making you look back at this week and you're seeing things differently," Saxby said. "How about farther back? Like, say, the past four to six months. Can you think of other days that were like what you just described, or times when you thought something was bothering him?"

"Hmmm, well, yes, I think so," Mrs. Hill said. "There were probably a handful of times when it seemed like something was weighing on him, but it's hard to define. I'm sure you know how it is when you're close to someone for years, you get to have a sense of when something's not right. You see, I enjoyed our visits, but also, because of our situation, I made a conscious effort to not pry. Or not much anyway. I didn't feel it was my business as much as it had been when we were married and living together. So, yes, Chief Saxby, if you asked me to pin it down, I'd have to say that something was hanging over him the last several months. Some big problem, or puzzle, or unwelcome change—I can't say, but I think there was something. And then there was the money."

"What do you mean by that?" Saxby said. "Was he having money problems? Asking you for money?"

"Oh no, that's not what I meant," Mrs. Hill said. "It's the opposite. It seemed like he had more money than ever before. Little things I noticed mostly, like splurging on a pricier bottle of wine than he would have in the past, or getting a big new TV when it wasn't strictly necessary. When we were together, we were fine. I've always had some family money, and he made a good salary. We were comfortable, but we didn't do flashy or extravagant things. I asked him about it once, after he bought that new car a few months ago and then started talking about one of those European river cruises. He told me he'd gotten a bigger raise then he expected and that a couple of stocks he'd bought years ago had finally paid off. He said he wanted to live a little. I just thought that was great and his explanation made sense to me. But looking back on all of it now, I'm not sure what to think. I'm starting to feel like I've been some kind of twit."

"Mrs. Hill, I really don't think you need to be so hard on yourself," Barstow said. "It seems to me like these little things you've noticed had reasonable explanations as they were happening. And some people are really good at hiding. It sounds like maybe your husband was one of those people."

"Thank you. That's nice of you to say that," Mrs. Hill said. She dabbed at her eyes with a handkerchief she'd taken out of her bag. "Do you think my husband was involved in something criminal? Was someone bribing him to do ... well ... what? I have no idea. He wasn't in any kind of powerful position as far as I know. This is all so crazy."

"Mrs. Hill, we aren't accusing your husband of anything right now," Saxby said, "but at this point we have to consider that he might have been involved in something bigger than simply doing his job at the lab. If I can switch gears for a minute, how long were you married to Dr. Hill?"

"Oh, I think it must be fifteen years," Mrs. Hill said. "Yes, that's right. We divorced two years ago, so right about seventeen since we got married."

"But you aren't originally from here though?" Saxby said. "Did I hear you mention that?"

"I don't remember if I mentioned it," Mrs. Hill said, "but no. Arthur and I met up in Montauk when he was doing research at a lab up there. It was a position not unlike what he's been doing here in Cape May. I can't remember the name of the place offhand, but he was there for at least ten years. We met at some marine conservation benefit event."

"I see. That's interesting," Saxby said. "And then after that he got the job down here and that's what brought you to Cape May?"

"Yes, that's right," Mrs. Hill said. "My parents had lived here for ages, and it was when we were in town visiting one time that he heard about the opening here at the marine center. It all happened quickly. They were glad to get him, we were happy to move here, and that's how we ended up in Cape May. That must have been seven or eight years ago."

"And as far as you know, did he stay in touch with anyone from his former employer in Montauk?" Saxby said.

"Not that I can recall," Mrs. Hill said, "but he might have. He left on good terms and had enjoyed working there."

"Okay, well, I think that's enough for today," Saxby said, standing up. "As long as we can find you if we have more questions. Thanks very much for coming in this morning, and once again, please accept our sympathies on your loss."

Barstow found Saxby in his office after escorting Mrs. Hill out. "You thinking what I'm thinking, Chief?"

"Probably, knowing you and knowing me," Saxby said. "I'm thinking somebody was paying him off to do something related to their research, but I don't know what it is yet. I'm interested to see how whatever Windsor Bell has to say about Hill stacks up against some of the things Mrs. Hill just told us."

"Well, if my first meeting with her is any indication," Barstow said, "we should just let her talk and I bet a lot's gonna come out."

"How long do we have before she gets here?" Saxby said.

Barstow checked her watch. "We're expecting her in about forty-five minutes."

"Okay, that's good," Saxby said. "I've got a little time to

do some research. Then let's plan to meet in the conference room again. I have a feeling it might be interesting."

Dr. Windsor Bell arrived at the station precisely on time, and was greeted by Doreen out at the front reception desk. Sergeant Barstow collected her a minute later and brought her back to the conference room, where Saxby was already seated.

"Good morning, Dr. Bell," Saxby said, "thank you for agreeing to come in to talk with us. I'm Chief Tate Saxby, and I know you've already met Sergeant Vicki Barstow here."

"Well, I suppose I didn't have much choice, did I?" Dr. Bell said.

"Actually, you did, Dr. Bell," Saxby said. "You are not under arrest and you are free to leave at any time, but we sure would appreciate it if you didn't do that. I know that Sergeant Barstow spoke with you last night and told you about the sudden death of Dr. Arthur Hill, which means that in the last five or six days, the two scientists you've worked with most closely have been killed. While you are not currently a suspect, this is an ongoing investigation with any number of possibilities and we could really use your help. At the moment, I consider you an important witness."

"You know what, then," Dr. Bell said, "I'm sorry for snapping at you like that. You're both just doing your jobs. I'm not one of those people who wears my emotions on my sleeve, but I really am devastated by what happened to Lewis, and now this news about Arthur last night that I'm still trying to believe. I keep it all inside and I make a joke or a snappy remark, and I'm sorry for that. I guess I'm in shock, and, you know, more than a little terrified."

"I'm sorry you're terrified, but I can certainly under-stand it," Saxby said. "If you help us, we'll do our best to help you." Saxby directed his next comment to Barstow. "You want to bring Dr. Bell up to date on what we discussed?"

"Sure, I'll be glad to do that," Barstow said. She took a moment to shuffle a few papers on the table in front of her before addressing Dr. Bell: "When I spoke with you last night, I told you that Dr. Hill had been killed in a fire in his garage, which appears to serve also as a sort of office. That's true as far as it goes, but there's more to it than that. What I didn't tell you is that we found a second body in that building with him."

"If I could just interject quickly," Saxby said, "bear in mind that much of what we're talking about today is part of an ongoing investigation, so a lot can change. This is what we know so far. Pardon the interruption. Go ahead, Vic."

"Right, thanks, Chief," Barstow said. "So, like the chief said, we're still putting the pieces together, but we believe that the second man found with Dr. Hill had come there to kill him. Came from out of town in fact. It looks like he succeeded in that, and then accidentally killed himself in his effort to start a fire to destroy the evidence."

Dr. Bell threw a hand up to cover her mouth as she recoiled back into her seat. "Somebody actually murdered him? And then burned the place down? Oh my God! Is this real?"

"I'm afraid it is, Dr. Bell," Barstow said. "We think this man came to town to locate and kill Dr. Hill. Exactly why is not something we know yet. Something else we want to tell you is about Dr. Forbes, who was attacked last Sunday night and died as a result of wounds received in that attack. I'll repeat that this is still under investigation, but we had reached the point that we considered Dr. Hill to be the most likely suspect in the attack on Dr. Forbes."

"Oh my God, this is all so unbelievable," Dr. Bell said. "I'm not sure which is more incredible, the idea that Arthur would have some reason to harm Lewis, or that someone would actually want to kill Arthur. That is what you're saying about what happened to Arthur, right? Like a hitman or something like that?"

"Well, remember, it's early in the investigation," Barstow said, "but yes, that is what it looks like. A hired killer, or someone with a grudge from his past ... we don't know yet."

"That's incredible. Just incredible. When I first met with you, Sergeant," Dr. Bell said, "and you told me about Lewis, I remember sharing with you my idea that someone might be out there trying to stop our research, but I didn't know who that was. Later, it occurred to me that you probably thought it was me who was 'out there,' you know, coming up with conspiracy theories. I must have sounded like a real nut case. At the time, I was reacting to the news about Lewis, but I really do think there's something there, though I can't define it. I feel it even more so now with all this you're telling me about Arthur."

"Dr. Bell, I respect the idea of a strong feeling that's hard to define," Saxby said. "I wouldn't dismiss it. At this point, if you would please, could you take a few minutes and describe for us what it was like to work with Dr. Hill? What I mean is, was he a person you would call a 'team player'? Did he get along with the others? With Lewis Forbes in particular?"

"Ah ... okay, sure," Dr. Bell said. "Let's see. Like many scientists, Arthur was a quiet man, but not in any kind of strange way. Like a lot of people in our line of work, he wasn't particularly outgoing, just more the kind of person to focus on his work and mind his own business. Lewis was the same way too, but they got along well as far as I knew. I got along with both of them equally. He was a well-meaning, hard-working man for the most part, but there was something different about him over the past few months, and I can't help but think that's part of my whole idea about something big going on with the research. Now, of course you're going to ask me how was he different, and I don't have a good answer. He was troubled about something. I'm sorry that's so vague."

"That's okay. We appreciate your openly sharing your impressions," Saxby said. "In fact, another person we spoke with recently described a similar feeling about Dr. Hill, as if maybe he was under some pressure that others didn't know about. Let me ask you something that might seem out of the blue: to your knowledge, how was he about money? Was that anything you ever talked about?"

"Money? Hmmm, no, not really," Dr. Bell said. "I mean, obviously everyone at the lab is a salaried worker and we probably know roughly how much everyone makes, but it isn't something that was openly discussed for the most part. Funny ... since you're asking and making me think about it though, there was one strange thing that happened a few months ago. A strange moment maybe. Arthur had just bought a new car—a really nice Audi. I couldn't say what model, but it wasn't one of the lower-end ones. I mean, I didn't really care about it, but I remember it because I had bought a new car that same weekend. I came in Monday with my new Honda Accord, which I was proud of and very excited about, and Arthur showed up with this new fancy Audi, which, I don't know, probably cost twice as much as my Honda. Like I said, I didn't really care, and anyway it's none of my business, but I made some comment, like 'Oh wow, here's Arthur with a fancy-shmancy Audi...' or something like that, and I think he was embarrassed about it. He said something about how his wife had given him some extra money towards the car. Again, I was just being friendly and making a little jab, but it turned awkward for a minute. I told him I was just kidding and I hope he enjoys his car, and that was it. We went on with our workday and that was the end of it. I only mention it because you asked about money. I can't think of anything else along that line. A Honda Accord is a really nice car, by the way."

"Yes, that's true," Saxby said. "A Honda Accord is a really good car. It should serve you well for years. So, basically, you made a little joke about the Audi and it appeared to hit a nerve with him, and he played it off by saying his wife had chipped in for it. Okay, then. You've mentioned this general perception you had about Dr. Hill that he was under some kind of unusual pressure over the past few months, or worried about something perhaps. Do you think that was affecting his work?"

"I'm not aware that it affected the quality of his work in any way," Dr. Bell said, "but our research was having its own ups and downs, which affected everyone to some degree. I'm sure you know what it's like to have a good day or a bad day at work. That happens to research scientists too."

"The work you were doing," Saxby said, "about the possibility of using something in scallops to help with treatments for Alzheimer's disease, how was that going—in your view?"

"Now, you need to know that research like that has been going on for years, in different parts of the country," Dr. Bell said. "Not simply for Alzheimer's but for other afflictions as well, and not only with scallops. In simple terms, it has to do with finding the right sequence of enzymes present in the flesh of the animal. For example, you could find enzyme A, and then enzyme B appears to be present, and you start to get excited, but then you can't find enzyme C and you have to start over."

"Excuse me just a second," Saxby said, "but just to make sure I'm following. You start over with looking at a different species of animal?"

"Very possibly a different species, sure," Dr. Bell said, "but that would be a major recalibration. A more likely adjustment might be to shift the research to looking at the same species but from a different environment. For example, horseshoe crabs from the Yucatan Peninsula in Mexico could be very different from the same species that lives along the Delaware Bay coast of New Jersey. I'm sure you know that horseshoe crab blood is used in vaccine testing."

"Oh, of course," Saxby said. "So, you were starting to talk about how the research was going before I interrupted you..."

"Right, so, the sort of research we do generally moves at a glacial pace," Dr. Bell said. "And this year has been no exception. Or at least the beginning of the year was that way. Frankly, if you had asked me in the first few months of the year if we were going to be successful, I'd have told you that I doubt it. At that time, I was at least halfway to thinking we'd all be working on something else soon. Then, it must have been about five or six months ago that we suddenly started getting some more favorable results. Somewhere around April or May. We got a new tub in that started to look very promising..."

"A new tub?" Barstow said. "Sorry, but what does that mean?"

"No, it's I who should be sorry," Dr. Bell said. "A new tub of Atlantic scallops. The lab contracts with a few local men who go around to various harbors and fisheries to collect the marine samples we need, such as a tub of scallops. I'm not sure what they call it—a bushel maybe, but it's a lot of scallops. I certainly can't pick it up. We keep them alive in our tanks at the center and use them as needed."

"Ah, interesting. Thanks for explaining that," Saxby said. "I'd appreciate if you could get us what information you have on those local fishermen. We might want to talk to them. So, testing for understanding once again, the research was moving along, if a bit of a slog, and then around mid or late spring you took in a shipment of scallops that started to give you some more exciting test results. Do I have that about right?"

"Yes, you've summed it up quite well," Dr. Bell said. "Bearing in mind that I've given you a highly abbreviated and simplified picture of the work we do. You've got the gist of it."

"Who at the marine center usually does the ordering?" Saxby said.

"Any of us can if we need to," Dr. Bell said. "But it was usually Arthur who handled that. He got us whatever we needed very efficiently. Here, I can look up the main fisherman contact for you." She took a moment to work with her phone before handing it to Barstow, who copied down a name and number from the screen.

"Thanks for that. You said something about how the sort of research you've been doing here is also done at other locations around the country," Saxby said. "To your knowledge, have any other facilities come close to finding what you're looking for? Like with the enzyme A, B, and C process?"

"A few have," Dr. Bell said. "Over the years, but as I mentioned earlier, it's a long slow process with a lot of ups and downs. Exciting possibilities that branch off to a dead end, if you will. That's the nature of much scientific research to a great extent. One of the facilities that came the closest, in terms of Alzheimer's disease was a lab not unlike ours on Gardiners Island, which is up in Long Island Sound. They got close, but ultimately had to move on to other areas of research for one reason or other. As a matter of fact, I'm pretty sure it was Arthur who told me about that, not long after he came to work with us.

Before he came to Cape May, he had worked at some other lab in that area. Maybe it was Montauk, but I'm not sure."

Saxby had been plowing through work at his desk for hours when he started to hear the various and familiar sounds of officers coming and going for a shift change, and he realized how late it was. After he and Sergeant Barstow had finished up with Dr. Windsor Bell, they had taken a half-hour to discuss the morning's two meetings and compare notes, before going their separate ways. Now, with the clock showing five o'clock, Barstow knocked on the open office door.

"Whew. I really lost track of time," Saxby said, "but I've been making some interesting progress. How about you?"

"Me too, I think," Barstow said, pulling a chair up to the corner of Saxby's desk and taking a seat. "I was able to get the warrant you asked for, so I'll start looking into Hill's finances right away. Right away after dinner I mean—I forgot to have lunch and I'm starved. Starved and beat."

"Me too, Vic, me too," Saxby said. "I'm interested to see what you find out about Hill's source of extra money. It had to be coming from somewhere."

"Right, and seems like it was some serious cash too" Barstow said. "He tells his ex-wife he got it from selling some old stocks, but turns around and tells Windsor Bell the money came from the ex-wife. Clearly hiding something there."

"Or maybe just embarrassed or ashamed about it for

some reason," Saxby said. "Were you able to look up that fisherman Bell told us about?"

"Yeah, it was pretty easy in fact," Barstow said. "Benny Morris is his name, and he usually works on one of the boats over near Two-Mile. Interesting thing is, he's got a few priors. Just minor drug stuff mostly, but I figure it might be enough to make sure he's inclined to answer a few questions if I go over to see him tomorrow morning."

"You're right, that could be a help," Saxby said. "I can't wait to hear what he says. That might fill in a piece or two of the puzzle."

At that moment, Doreen poked her head in the door. "Sorry to interrupt, Chief, but you asked me to let you know as soon as I got that info you asked for."

"Great, thanks, Doreen," Saxby said. "That was fast. What did you find?"

"It's registered to a company, not a person," Doreen said. "With an address on Landis Avenue at the north end of Sea Isle. TOWSON Investments, as in Towson, Maryland, I suppose. Here, I wrote it all down for you." She handed Saxby a sheet of paper and went out.

Saxby looked at the paper for a moment. "I think I'll be heading up to Sea Isle to check this out, but that's gonna have to wait for Monday morning. Looks like we've got good weather for Oktoberfest tomorrow. How are we set for that?"

"I believe we're in good shape on that, Chief," Barstow said. "Three's been working with the chamber for a good chunk of the last few days and he thinks we're ready. It'll be all hands on deck for us. Plus, we'll have all the usual volunteers to handle the vendors and parking and all that stuff. Should be a good crowd and it's good for the town."

"You're right, it's very good for the town and the visitors," Saxby said. "It's a long day, but hopefully an uneventful one. I order you to try to take a mental break from all this and enjoy walking around and talking to the people. That's what I'm going to try to do."

"Yeah, well, I'll do my best," Barstow said. She stood up and moved towards the door. "Okay, Chief, I think I'll head back to my desk to put in another hour or two, then home for some dinner."

"Sounds like a good plan, Vic," Saxby said. "And about the same as mine. I'll be here for another hour or so. Angela's working late at the Mug and I'm overdue to pop in. If you feel like coming by later, say eight-ish, drinks are on me."

17

S axby arrived at the Ugly Mug at eight sharp. Knowing that it was the night before the big Okto-berfest event in town, he was not surprised to find the place doing a brisk business, but he was still able to get one of his favorite booths in the corner near the bar. In honor of the special weekend, the DJ was doing an '80s night theme, and was keeping the customers happy with a selection of old hits that Saxby knew from his own party days as a much younger man out and about in town.

"Double bourbon on the rocks for you, Chief?" the waitress asked, when she came up a minute after he sat down.

"You know, Wendy, that does sound good," Saxby said, "but the long day I'm looking at tomorrow is telling me to stick to beer tonight. How about a Sam seasonal in honor of Oktoberfest, and a basket of those garlic parmesan fries if we still have some."

"Got it, Chief," Wendy said. "And shall I tell the manager you're here or are you incognito?"

"That would be great, thanks. If she's not too busy," Saxby said. "You might as well ask her if she wants a drink too."

Saxby's beer arrived a few minutes later, along with a glass of a chilled white wine. He took a few sips of the wine, considering it carefully, before moving on to his frosty mug of beer. He had drunk a quarter of it when his fiancée appeared at the table along with the fries.

"I hear you ordered a basket of fries and demanded to speak to the manager," Angela said, sitting down across from him while working to keep a straight face. "And it looks like someone's stolen some of my wine. I might have to call the police."

"Oh, don't bother," Saxby said. "You know how the police are. It'll take them forever to get here. Actually, maybe if they heard about these fries, they'd come rushing over."

"Speaking of the police rushing right over," Angela said, "I guess Vic must have heard about the fries, because here she comes."

"Hey, Ang, Chief," Barstow said. She slipped into the booth across from Saxby after Angela stood up to let her in. "I always feel like I'm butting in on you two when I come in, yet I still do it."

"I invited you, Vic," Saxby said. "I would only do that if I wanted you to show up."

"I second that," Angela said. "It's good to see you. It's been a while. Nice to see you out in your civvies." She made a gesture to indicate Barstow's casual attire of faded blue jeans, light sweater, and well-worn leather bomber jacket.

"My uniform is comfortable," Barstow said, "but it's still great to take a shower and put on some soft old jeans. What is that you're drinking, Ang? I was thinking it was a night for wine."

Angela waved to get the attention of the waitress as she pushed her wine glass closer to Barstow. "It's an un-oaked chardonnay that we just got in. Sonoma Coast. It's a little young, but I like it a lot. Great for a fall evening."

Barstow nodded in approval after taking a sip as the waitress came over. "Mmmm, that is very nice. I'll have a glass of that."

"Bring us a new bottle of this please, Wendy," Angela said. "And another glass for Vic here."

"Oh, we don't need a whole bottle, do we?" Barstow said. "I mean, I might have a second glass, but…"

"It's fine, Vic, have whatever you like," Angela said. "If we don't finish it, you'll take it home."

"Leaving a bar with an open bottle, I don't know," Barstow said. "That's probably against the law."

"Vic, I'm the chief of police," Saxby said, "and I say … enjoy that wine."

"Got it, boss, whatever you say," Barstow said. The wine arrived a minute later, along with a table-top ice bucket, and Saxby topped up Angela's glass before pouring one for Barstow.

"I hope you didn't work too late," Saxby said. "Anything new I should know about?"

"Actually, there is a little news that I wanted you to know right away," Barstow said, "which is what made me decide to get it together to come out tonight. Is it okay to talk about it here?"

Saxby knew that what she meant was 'is it okay to talk about the case in front of Angela?' Before answering, he let his eyes take a spin around the room and the nearby tables and bar. "It's fine, Vic. Angela's mostly up to date on the case anyway. As long as it's okay with her, it's okay with me."

"It's okay with me," Angela said. "I like to hear all the exciting developments. With everything that goes on right here in town, I think I might just cancel my Netflix subscription."

"Okay, as long as you say so, though some of it might be unpleasant," Barstow said. "At least we have a whole bottle of wine."

"The first thing is, we got the report from the medical examiner on the two men in the fire—Dr. Hill and the other guy, Jack Rhodes. I can say Jack Rhodes for sure now because Dr. Coyle was able to get dental records today and he says that's the guy. That, the wallet, the engraved watch, and the car all say he's Jack Rhodes of Port Jefferson, New York. They plan to release the body to the family on Tuesday because there's nothing more they need to do with it. No idea who 'the family' is."

"That all happened fast," Saxby said. "But good for us. Did we get confirmation on cause of death for both men?"

Barstow took another look around before continuing as quietly as possible. "Yes, Dr. Hill was killed by a .38 caliber bullet to the back of the head, with the bullet matching the Colt Detective Special that Rhodes had on him. His burn injuries were post-mortem. For Rhodes, it was trauma and tissue damage from the burns."

"So, he was burned alive," Angela said. "That's horrible."

"Yes, it is horrible," Saxby said. "The whole situation is horrible, but thanks for summing it up, Vic. I'll read the full report over the weekend. What else you got?"

"The other thing is easier to talk about, so it's downhill from here," Barstow said. "On a whim after I left the office, I went over to the docks and found Benny Morris without much trouble at all. You know, the local guy who was one of the people who supplied the research lab with the scallops they needed for their experiments. I didn't need to lean on him much at all. I guess with his record, he was nervous enough to have a police officer come up to talk to him, and after I told him we were working on a homicide case involving Dr. Hill and the lab, he was all ready to give me his grandmother's blood type or whatever."

"Good work, sounds like you played it well," Saxby said. "What'd you find out?"

"He confirmed for me that late last April," Barstow said, "Dr. Hill asked him for a standard tub of scallops, but not from the waters around here. Hill specifically wanted scallops from Long Island Sound near New London. Morris told me he didn't like it and refused to do it at first, until Hill offered him five hundred bucks extra and assured him it was a one-time thing. He went up there, got the scallops, and delivered them to the lab in the same type of container they usually used, so everyone would think they were local to South Jersey."

"Wow. That's big. Really big," Saxby said. "Things are starting to come into focus."

"But what does all that mean, Tate?" Angela said. "Why bring in scallops from somewhere else?"

"I think I've got it," Saxby said. "Or at least I think I'm

getting it. Keep me straight on this, Vic. So, one of the other scientists who worked with them—Windsor Bell is her name, Ang—told us their research was kind of plodding along early this year until around April when they got a new shipment of scallops in. That's when they started to get some more exciting results. Gave a shot in the arm to their research, I guess. Then, a month, maybe six weeks ago, is when Lewis Forbes secretly ordered a smaller sample of scallops from the same area of Long Island Sound. Not long after that, he made a reference in his journal that suggested he needed to confront Arthur Hill about something."

"And he did confront Hill," Barstow said, "presumably, or the other way around, and then within a week or two Forbes was dead."

"Right. So, here's how I see it..." Saxby said. He sat back and waited a moment while the waitress delivered a fresh beer and poured some more wine for the two ladies. "Going back about eight years, Arthur Hill worked at a lab in Montauk, where they were doing research similar to what they've been doing here in Cape May. Their research got close but eventually the people at that lab gave up. Early this year, the research here in Cape May wasn't going much of anywhere. For reasons we don't know yet, Hill hired local gopher Benny Morris to bring in a tub of scallops from a supplier in New London. In other words, he brought in some of the scallops that he remembered had given some promising results years ago in Montauk. I don't know the 'why' yet, but Hill was being paid by someone to skew the research."

"Or, you know what, Chief," Barstow said. "Maybe what

he was trying to do was to drag the research out. Like, maybe he was worried they'd give up soon but he didn't want it to end yet."

"That's a good idea, Vic," Saxby said. "Good possibility. Only, my thought on that is that it wasn't Hill, but whoever was paying Hill who didn't want the project to end yet. I'm betting Hill was a pawn in the whole thing. In any case, it must have been around late August or thereabouts that Lewis Forbes somehow figured out that he'd been working on scallops from Long Island Sound all summer. Or at least he suspected it. That's why he ordered the small sample of scallops from New London to confirm they were exactly the same. He must have been furious at Hill and wanted to confront him with the whole thing. Maybe they talked about it a few times. But then last Sunday came along, with Hill going over to see Forbes at his house. Things get heated, with Forbes threatening to expose Hill for faking the research."

"And Hill loses it and whacks Forbes on the head with the Bunsen burner," Barstow said. "But why? I mean, why was someone paying Hill to try to interfere with the research?"

"Right, why? That's what I haven't figured out yet," Saxby said. "But now that we have the warrant, make it a priority to look into his finances. Hopefully that'll tell us where all his extra money was coming from. Follow the money and, with luck, everything else will start to fall into place."

Saxby sat back and took a long slug of his beer just as Mark Allen came up to the table, pausing there for a moment as he put on his coat. "Oh, hey, Mark, you on your way out?"

"Yeah, it's been a long day," Allen said, "and with Oktoberfest going on, tomorrow's gonna be longer. I'll be manning the radio station booth all day."

"Got ya. I'll be sure to stop by," Saxby said. "We'll be there all day too, Vic and I and the whole department, wandering around. Looks like the weather should be pretty good, last time I looked."

"That's what we want," Allen said. "Good enough so we don't get rained on and people want to go outside, but not so good that people go sit on the beach. Hey, I heard about that fire last night. Really terrible."

"You got that right, Mark," Saxby said. "We're still trying to figure out if it was an accident or what. Don't know how it happened yet."

"Well, look, I'm interrupting you and it's time for me to get going," Allen said, after giving Saxby a look that lasted an extra two seconds. "Maybe we can have breakfast again soon and you can fill me in on whatever you can share."

"That sounds great, Mark," Saxby said. "Give me a few more days and I'm sure there'll be plenty to talk about." He returned Allen's look, adding his own extra second.

"Well then, goodnight, folks," Allen said, through a wide grin. "Be sure to stop by the booth tomorrow."

"I think he's got the right idea," Angela said, as Mark Allen walked away. "I'm about to fall into my wine. How about taking me home soon, Chief Saxby."

"Yeah, I'm tired too," Barstow said. "Early start tomorrow and I'd like to feel good. Oh, and look—we killed the wine, so I don't have to worry about getting busted on the way home. How convenient."

18

Saturday came early for the police, firefighters, and other city employees who worked together to plan and coordinate the Oktoberfest activities that sprawled across the center of town in and around the three-block pedestrian shopping area known familiarly as "the mall." By eight o'clock, volunteers with clipboards were busily directing merchandise vendors to their assigned spots, where they rushed to unload their wares and set up tents and tables, all while munching on breakfast sandwiches and washing them down with large coffees from the Wawa or their favorite local café.

Food trucks parked in their designated places and began the well-rehearsed routine of setting up and getting ready to serve piles of grilled kielbasa, pork sandwiches, giant pretzels, and funnel cakes to the expected crowds. Two local breweries were getting ready to serve plastic cups of beer to thirsty revelers in the roped-off beer garden that anchored the end of the row of food trucks.

"I never have figured out why they call it a beer garden," Barstow said, as she and Saxby passed the display for Cape May Brewery. I mean, it seems like every one I've ever seen is either on a street, like here, or in some ugly parking lot."

"I guess the original idea is that a pub would have a little grassy area outside where you could sit with your beer," Saxby said. "I bet that's it. Angela calls it a 'garden of beer.' As long as everyone keeps it within the event, they can call it whatever they want. Hey, there's Starla's tent. Want a coffee or something?"

Saxby could tell that Starla, as the main baker for Starla's Cafe, must have been up well before the crack of dawn —based on the wide array of scones, cookies, and other temptations that were on display. Barstow ordered a latte, while Saxby took a regular coffee, both making a careful choice of cookie. With Starla herself not in evidence, Saxby spoke briefly with the young woman who appeared to be in charge of sales before coming back to Barstow to resume their tour. "I told her if anyone from the department comes by for a coffee and a baked something or other, to just keep a running tally and I'll take care of it at the end of the day. Maybe you could spread the word to the troops."

"That's very nice of you, Chief," Barstow said, "and thank you. I'll let people know."

For the next thirty minutes, the two of them walked the several blocks that served as the event area, stopping frequently to chat with various vendors and volunteer workers. As they walked, they made use of a few quiet moments to discuss the case.

"Now that the ME's report is out," Barstow said, "I guess it's going to come out that the fire wasn't an accident."

"You're right, Vic," Saxby said. "But at least it's the weekend, so we should be able to keep it under wraps till Monday morning. I'll talk to Mark Allen today and tell him it's okay for the *Star & Wave* to know about it starting Monday. Then the cat will be out of the bag and we'll have to deal with it. We don't need our Oktoberfest visitors freaking out about a bunch of murders in town this week, now do we?"

As they came upon the booth for WCFA radio, and saw Mark Allen laying out an assortment of promotional materials for the station, Saxby told Barstow to go on ahead without him. "Let me talk to Mark for a few while it's still quiet and I'll catch up with you after." He went over to Allen's table while she continued the tour alone.

"Good morning, Mark," Saxby said. "Seems like I haven't seen you in hours."

"Morning to you, Chief Saxby," Allen said. "How's the patrol going so far?"

"Well, it's early, but things seem to be well organized, and it should warm up into a very nice fall day," Saxby said. "But, Mark, I need to ask you a favor."

"Don't worry about it, Tate," Allen said. "I can keep a secret well as anyone else. Though you should know I have friends in the fire department." He followed that with an exaggerated wink.

"I know you do," Saxby said. "I know I could never pull one over on you, and I appreciate your help. The ME's report got done in a flash, but now it's the weekend and this right here is the big thing in town, so how about Monday morning for the *Star & Wave*? What I'm saying is, I really want the fire to stay an accident until Monday morning. After that, it can be in the next paper, or the radio—whatever. As a matter of fact, we'll do the standard news release, so the *AC Press* will probably run it first."

"I'm on board with all of that," Allen said. "But you'll owe me that breakfast soon and I'll need to hear all the juicy details."

"You've got yourself a deal there," Saxby said. "And thanks a lot. I'll talk to the fire chief today and make sure we're on the same page."

"I've known Barney a long time," Allen said. "I'm sure he won't have any problem playing along."

"Thanks, Mark," Saxby said. "Now I'd better keep moving along and check in with the crew. Catch you again soon."

Saxby continued down the road, chatting with the vendors and the food truck people as he went, until reconnecting with Barstow twenty minutes later. After they walked together for a while, he looked at his watch. "It looks like everything's under control here, Vic. I'm going to go back to the station and spend a few hours at my desk. There's a couple of things I'd like to dig into. Call me if you need me, but otherwise I'll be back by about two. Make sure you and all the others fit in a break, okay? You're in charge, but maybe try to enjoy yourself a little bit too."

〜

It was shortly after he had come back to the Oktoberfest event that Saxby bought a lemonade from one of the food vendors. As he turned away after paying, he had to stop himself quickly to avoid spilling the lemonade all over a tall man who'd been passing.

"Chief Saxby, isn't it?" the man said, himself recovering from the near mishap. "Brewster Atwater—we met a few days ago at my office. Nice to see you again."

"Yes, of course, I'm sorry for that near miss, Mr. Atwater," Saxby said. "Even the police chief needs to look where he's going. Are you enjoying Oktoberfest?"

"Yes, I think I am in fact," Atwater said. "I was just at a meeting in town with an old friend, and we thought, why not have a look around and maybe even try some of that … oh, what is it called? That's right—street food. Isn't that what you call it when you buy a sandwich from one of these trucks? So many good smells."

Saxby allowed himself a small laugh. "Yes, that's right. 'Street food' is a common term at events like this. Many of these trucks are run by professional chefs who have successful restaurants of their own, so there's bound to be some good food here."

"Well then, I'm going to try some, and it will be a new experience for me," Atwater said. "Tell me, Chief Saxby, how is your investigation going? That matter with the scientist."

"It's moving along slowly," Saxby said. "Which is generally the way these things go. It's really only on TV that cases are neatly resolved within a few hours."

"I'm sure the reality is that it's a gradual and careful

process," Atwater said. He shifted to one side in order to gesture to a man who'd been standing behind him. "Ah, there you are. Chief Saxby, this is the old friend I mentioned, Bruce Devere. Bruce is what you'd call an 'oil man' going way back. Despite our different fields, we've been friends since too far back to remember."

"I'm pleased to meet you, Mr. Devere," Saxby said, shaking Devere's hand. "Are you from around here, or just visiting?"

"Oh, I'm in the area frequently, visiting friends or taking care of business," Devere said. "I have an apartment in North Wildwood and an office in Marmora, but I spend most of my time in the New York area. As you can probably guess by looking at me, I'm a bit long in the tooth to be hanging around the beach."

"Well, you have good timing this weekend," Saxby said, "with all this going on. Will you be staying in the area for the weekend?"

"I have some business to take care of on Tuesday," Devere said, "and then back north after that."

"Well, it was a pleasure meeting you, and I hope your Tuesday business goes well, Mr. Devere," Saxby said, turning back to Atwater. "I should let you both go so you can get your street food, but it was nice to see you again. Oh—I almost forgot—how did your meeting go? Was it that one out at the Cape May Point Science Center? Isn't that a great building? It was a nun's retreat for ages."

"Yes, that's the one, it's a fascinating facility," Atwater said. "And the meeting was very interesting. Time well spent I'd say, but now it's time for some grilled processed meat on a roll, don't you agree, Bruce?"

Saxby laughed, and with a final handshake, turned and left the other two men to search for new culinary experiences. *Bruce Devere. Hmmm. An interesting man,* he thought to himself. *Very charming, despite all that pain written across his face.*

A little later, after making another circuit through the festivities, Saxby used his cell phone to call Doreen back at the station.

"Afternoon, Chief," Doreen said, "is everything going alright over there at the mall?"

"All fine here so far," Saxby said. "It's a well-behaved crowd, and I think the vendors are doing well, so no complaints. I've resisted the giant bacon on a stick so far, but we'll see how long that lasts. Do you have time to look into a few things for me?"

"I've been mostly just catching up on all the filing and sorting," Doreen said, "so sure, I can handle something else. I'll grab a notepad."

"Fantastic. Just a few things," Saxby said. "First, find out what, if anything, is going on out at the Science Center at the Point. What time, what it's about, whatever you can dig up. The next thing is related. Put together a list of whatever's going on in town that you might call a meeting. Classes, lectures, business briefings in rented spaces, anything like that, okay? I know it's Saturday, and Oktoberfest is the big event today, so I don't think it'll be a very long list. I think it would likely be walking distance to the mall."

"Got it, Chief," Doreen said. "I'll work on that right away. Is there anything else?"

"That's good for the moment," Saxby said. "There's a

few other things I'd like you're help with, but we can talk about that later."

After hanging up with Doreen, Saxby resumed his patrol of the event, trying not to think about a giant slab of bacon on a stick.

19

By eleven o'clock Monday morning, Saxby had already been working at his desk for what seemed like most of a day. Getting into the office while the sky was still dark, he had fired up the coffee machine and set to work. For the better part of the last two hours, knowing that people on normal schedules had started to appear at their own places of work, he had been working the phone. After calls to the county detective office, the state police of both New Jersey and New York, and an old friend at the State Department, he was talked out and ready for a break and some fresh air. He figured it was a good time for a drive up to Sea Isle City, where he could drop in at the office of TOWSON Investments on the pretense of asking whoever was there if they had any ideas about opposition to wind farm construction. His plan was to ask for the manager, play a little bit dumb, and shake the tree to see whatever might fall out.

Thirty minutes later, he crossed the bridge onto the narrow barrier island that was home to Sea Isle City, and

made the left to go north along the main road. As the
northern part of town narrowed to just two blocks wide,
he easily found the small plaza with a pizza parlor and a
half-dozen other businesses that was his landmark before
the two-story office building just beyond it on the same
side. Slowing down almost to a stop to let a delivery van
pull out of the plaza, he saw a cobalt blue car pull out onto
the road a hundred yards ahead, proceeding north and
clearly driven by someone with a heavy foot. With the
delivery van out of the way, he proceeded past the plaza
and pulled into the lot for the office building, parking near
a sign that listed the several occupants, including
TOWSON Investments, on the second floor.

He waited a full minute before getting out of the car,
considering the correct course of action, until he was
struck with a fresh idea.

He took the flight of cement steps up to the second
floor, where twenty feet down an outside walkway was a
door marked TOWSON Investments. He opened the door
and went in, finding himself in a neat, generic-looking
waiting area, where the usual grouping of chairs, small
tables, and stacks of popular business magazines were
overseen by a reception desk with no visible receptionist.
There were doors on either side of the wall behind the
desk, and after about twenty seconds, the one on the left
opened and a casually dressed thirtyish woman came out.

"Oh, I'm sorry, Officer, I didn't realize you had come in.
The buzzer must be on the fritz again. I'm afraid the
manager just left a few minutes ago and I'm here by myself.
Is there something I can help you with?"

"No need to be sorry, I haven't been here very long at

all," Saxby said. "And darn it, just my luck with the bad timing. I'm not here on official business, just some personal investing questions. I've inherited some money and I'm starting to look into what's the right thing to do with it. Does your firm handle private clients?"

"We do, but I'm very sorry," she said, "we aren't taking on any clients at this time. We're working to transition to new strategies, so they've put a freeze on new accounts. I might be able to recommend somewhere else if you'd like."

"Hmmm, I'm sorry to hear that," Saxby said, "but don't bother with that for now. I'm just kicking ideas around at this stage. I'm meeting with someone tomorrow who should be able to point me in the right direction. Thanks for the offer though. Have a good day."

Saxby left and went back down to his car. If someone had bumped into him in the parking lot just then, they might have wondered why he was smiling to himself.

Back on the mainland, Saxby turned right when he hit Route 9 to head north towards the town of Marmora. Less than ten minutes later, he pulled into the parking lot of the local office of DelVal United, which he knew to be one of the largest refinery supply and maintenance companies on the East Coast. The single-story brick building appeared to be a busy place, with at least ten cars parked outside. The receptionist was engaged in an animated phone call that sounded to Saxby to be something about an order for large-diameter PVC piping. She gave him a wave and pointed to the phone. Behind the receptionist's desk was a double sliding window, through which Saxby could see part of a cubicle-filled office that looked like it might support about a dozen people. The receptionist was still well into her phone call when Saxby saw a somewhat frail-looking older man on the other side of the glass, appearing to speak with someone who was not in view. The man talked for half a minute before turning to look out through the glass at the reception area, spotting Saxby. After holding up a finger, the man disappeared from view, only to emerge from a door in the corner into the reception area. "Saxby, isn't it?" the man said. "Didn't we meet the other day? Yes, Saturday, at that street fair in Cape May. I'm sure of it."

"Your memory is correct, Mr. Devere," Saxby said, shaking Devere's hand. "Chief Tate Saxby of the Cape May police."

"Ah, I thought so. Other ailments aside, my memory still serves me well," Devere said. "Brewster introduced us. He told me that you had interviewed him at his office earlier in the week regarding the scientist who was killed. Is that what you came all the way up here to see me about?"

"Actually, it was more spur-of-the-moment than that," Saxby said. "I had another appointment in Sea Isle City that was cut short, and I thought if I managed to find your office up here you might spare me a few minutes. I thought it could be helpful to our investigation to get your take on some of what Mr. Atwater and I discussed the other day. I won't take more than ten or fifteen minutes of your time if you can spare it. Is there somewhere we can talk?"

"Yes, of course," Devere said. "I'm happy to help in any way I can. Let's go back to my office."

He led Saxby back through the door from the reception area to a spacious office to one side of the open cubicle area, closing the door behind them. He gestured to a pair of upholstered chairs sitting across from one another to one side of his desk.

"This scientist who was killed," Devere said, "Forbes, I think is what I heard. Brewster told me you had the idea that it might have something to do with someone wanting to prevent some big wind farm from being built off the coast near here. Is that right?"

"That's one idea I've been working on," Saxby said. "But also, I'm not ruling out someone who was 'pro-wind farm.' Meaning, someone who might want to interfere with the research going on at the Cape Shore Marine Research Center, in order somehow to make approval of the wind farm more likely. I consider both to be possibilities."

"But how would either of those scenarios be advanced by killing one of the scientists?" Devere said. "That does seem rather like a 'bull in a China shop' approach."

"I like your metaphor there," Saxby said, "and yes, that is one of the puzzles I keep coming back to. But that's my job to keep working on that. If we could set that aside for the moment, when I met with Mr. Atwater last week, I asked him to give me his general impressions about opposition to or support for wind farms from the point of view of the fishing industry. I wanted to 'take the temperature' basically. When he introduced you, he called you an 'oil man', so, I'd like to ask you for the same, but from the perspective of the fossil fuel side of things. How do people in your industry feel about wind farms being built? Fearful? Threatened maybe? I don't know, which is why I'm here.

I'd be grateful for any impressions you'd be willing to share."

"Well, I'm happy to share my impressions," Devere said, "but I don't know how helpful I'll be. It's a vast industry and I'm just a small piece of it."

"I think you're being modest there, Mr. Devere," Saxby said. "I have a longstanding habit—appropriate for my job, I think—of doing a little research on people I plan to meet with. I realize you aren't ExxonMobil, but still, DelVal United is one of the biggest players on the East Coast in the refinery business. I'm sure you must have some good insights into the industry."

"Well, as I said, I'm happy to try to help," Devere said. "Hmmm. Let me think. It's true that I know many other people in my line, and it's also true that in recent years there's been plenty of grumbling about wind energy. The same is true for solar or any other type of new technology. Lots of people want things to always be the way they were."

"I thought you'd probably say something like that. That's not surprising," Saxby said. "What's your personal take on it? The wind farm, I mean."

"My personal take on it," Devere said, after chewing the question over for a moment, "is that I don't like it. This country was built on gasoline, coal, and diesel, and I think we're rushing into all this new gee-whiz stuff too fast. And anyway, the government shouldn't be involved in it at all. You know, picking sides. They shouldn't be dishing out huge grants for things that aren't perfected yet."

"Thanks for that clear answer," Saxby said. "Is it safe to say that many people share those views?"

"It is, but here's the thing, Chief Saxby," Devere said, "I'll tell you the same thing that I know Brewster told you, because he told me about it. That is, the future is coming at us like a freight train, whether we like it or not. What is it Doris Day was always singing about? That's right—whatever will be will be, or something like that. I think most mature people think that way."

"I tend to hope so," Saxby said. "Alright, well thank you for that. And you're right, that is pretty much the way Mr. Atwater put it too. Now, I'm going to shift gears to a subject you probably weren't aware of because the news was only released today. Lewis Forbes is not the only scientist from the lab in Cape May to be killed last week."

"Oh my God. That's so terrible," Devere said. He took a moment for a few breaths before continuing. It seemed to Saxby that his emotional reaction was genuine. "There's been another murder? What was the man's name?"

"His name was Dr. Arthur Hill," Saxby said. "And yes, it's definitely murder, and appears to be connected to the death of Dr. Lewis Forbes several days before. Did you know Dr. Hill, by any chance? Because before he came to Cape May eight years ago, he worked at the South Fork Marine Research Lab in Montauk. Isn't that somewhere you've spent a lot of time?"

Devere took some time before answering. Saxby again saw a wave of emotion cross his face. "Well, you really did do your research, didn't you, Chief Saxby? Yes, I knew Arthur back then, in Montauk. My wife and I used to rent a house there regularly, and it was always a favorite place. We first met at a benefit for the marine lab. I was one of their top donors, and he was one of the lead scientists, so naturally we got to talking over glasses of wine and hit it off. We were never close friends, and didn't travel in the same circles, but the few times we bumped into each other it was always good to catch up. I had a lot of respect for his knowledge and talent, and he had a lot of respect for my checkbook. That's not … I'm sorry. I didn't mean to be flippant. He was a good man and he worked hard. We fell out of touch after he and his wife moved down to Cape May."

"So, that was it, then? You never saw him after that?" Saxby said.

"No, not that I can recall," Devere said. "I think the last time I saw Arthur was at a restaurant in Amagansett. It was just a hello in passing, I hope you're well, enjoy your dinner sort of thing."

"I see. You're saying you lost touch with Dr. Hill when he went to work with the lab in Cape May," Saxby said. "Did you have any relationship with the lab there? The Cape Shore Marine Research Center?"

"I assume you mean as a donor," Devere said. "No, I was never involved with them, though I understand they're trying to do some good work."

"Yes, I believe they are," Saxby said. "Well then, Mr. Devere, I think I've taken enough of your time for now. I remember you said you have some business in the area tomorrow—will you be heading back to New York after that?"

"Yes, for a few days," Devere said. "I'll be coming back by the weekend for a get-together with some friends."

"Oh, that sounds nice," Saxby said. "Well, I'll let you get on with your day. I do appreciate you candidly sharing all of this. It could be a help with the case. Thanks."

As both men rose from their chairs, Saxby noticed a

pained look on Devere's face as he clutched his midsection for a few seconds.

"Are you okay, Mr. Devere?" Saxby said. "For a moment there you looked like you were in a lot of pain. Is there something I can do?"

Devere took a long, deep breath before waving the idea of help away. "Thank you, but I'll be fine. The pain can hit unexpectedly, but my doctors and I are working on it. Would you mind seeing yourself out, Chief Saxby? It's time for my pills and a little quiet time for me."

After shaking hands, Saxby left and went out to the reception area, where he was mildly surprised to see that the receptionist was no longer on the phone.

"I don't mean to butt in," Saxby said, "but you might want to check on Mr. Devere in a little while. Just as I was leaving, he seemed to be in a lot of pain. He said he was going to take some medication and relax for a bit, so I hope it passes. My uncle had stomach cancer too, and I remember that look of pain. Shame."

"Oh, thanks for letting me know," the receptionist said. "I'll check on him. It's pancreatic actually, for a few years now, but he's doing everything he can do to fight it."

"Oh, I'm sorry to hear that," Saxby said. "That's a tough hand to be dealt. But, as I said, I didn't mean to butt in. Just thought I'd pass that on. Have a good day now."

20

"You had an interesting morning, Chief," Barstow said. "Like you hoped for, it looks like some of the pieces are falling into place."

"They are, and it's about time too, isn't it?" Saxby said. "I got some good information from both of my stops, though I'm a little worried about becoming too good of a liar."

"Hey, you were just gathering information," Barstow said. "Not looking for anything to take in front of a jury. Ask a question, sit back and let people talk. You know who taught me that?"

"Yeah, that seems like something I would say, doesn't it?" Saxby said. "And many's the time I've been surprised at how well it works."

After leaving the office of DelVal United, Saxby had grabbed a sandwich at a nearby takeout place and eaten it in the car on the way back to Cape May. He'd found Barstow at her desk and together they'd walked the two blocks over to Starla's Café, where they caught each other up over cups of strong coffee.

"Let's go over what we know about Devere at this point," Saxby said. "I'll start. He knew Arthur Hill personally when they were both up in Montauk, and Hill worked at the research lab there. They were acquainted for at least a few years. Devere says that ended when Hill moved down here."

"But we know that isn't true," Barstow said, "because now we know he made at least four large deposits to Hill's bank account through two shell companies. Also, there's all the phone calls Hill made to Devere."

"Right, the phone calls. And a hundred grand is serious money," Saxby said. "But what really bent him was probably those corporate bonds we found in his papers. If DelVal United did well in the next three years, he could have cashed out over a million bucks."

"I'm guessing that's what Hill wanted. He wanted to cash out big," Barstow said. "He toiled away for years until he finally saw a way to have a fancy car and a European vacation. Maybe he felt it was his due."

"I'm sure you're right," Saxby said. "That's got to be what convinced him to spike the research. But Devere is more complicated. For him, it's a story about losing money and power."

"And that's the other thing we know about Devere," Barstow said, "he's strapped. I mean, strapped in his own rich guy level of being strapped. He's busily trying to sell off assets."

"I have a theory and I want you to tell me honestly what

you think of it," Saxby said. He looked into the dregs of his coffee for a moment. "Since Gerry Harmon told me about this gang of rich men he calls 'the power brokers', we've spoken to three of them, Atwater, Vaughn, and now Devere, and they clearly do have a connection, almost like an old-boys club or something. When I look at them, and I look at the attack on Lewis Forbes and then Arthur Hill, my natural first thought is that, somehow, they're trying to stop the wind farm. But then, when I step back and look at it with a little distance, I can't see how that makes any sense. Something I noticed today was that Devere was the first one of them to really come out and say how much he was against wind farm construction. Sure, he said 'the future is coming and I have to accept it, blah, blah, blah,' but I could see how much he hated it. He's a dying man and he's seeing his old-school businesses struggle. I think that, aside from lip service, he's not as accepting of the future that's coming down the road as his friends are. I think he got in touch with his old friend Dr. Arthur Hill and convinced him to find a way to drag out the research, giving him more time to divest himself of some of his refinery-related properties. From talking with Windsor Bell and seeing all that stuff Clemson Colson found in Forbes' notes, my guess is that the ruse was going fine until Forbes stumbled on the fact that they were working on scallops from Long Island Sound. Hill tried to manage that situation, but it didn't go very well, ending up with Forbes dead on the floor. That's when Hill freaked out and started calling Devere."

"And after a couple of days of that," Barstow said, "Devere found someone to come down to Cape May to contain the situation—someone he thought was 'a tough guy'—and that was Jack Rhodes. I wonder if Rhodes was only supposed to pay Hill off, or maybe twist his arm a little. We'll never know."

"That could be it. Yeah, it's possible," Saxby said. "But let's remember that Rhodes showed up at Hill's house with a gun and a box of Molotov cocktails. Still, he might have intended to start with a softer approach. You're right that we'll never know, because they're both dead. It makes me uneasy when the person you're sure is the killer is killed, and unanswered questions get left behind. I hate that."

"I know, Chief," Barstow said, "but we do the best we can with what we have. Your theory makes a lot of sense to me. It fits the facts, and accounts for Hill's motivations and Forbes' death. So, what's next?"

"I have a strong feeling this is coming to a head, Vic," Saxby said, "but we have a few more things to do. I'd like you to check out a boat called the *Bonnie Marie*. It's some kind of party rental boat or something like that. Probably very high-end. Find out anything you can about it as soon as possible, and I'll explain everything later."

"Okay ... check out a party boat. I'll get right on that," Barstow said. "And how about you?"

"What I'm going to do next is to dig into Trans-Oceanic Wind," Saxby said. "I need to go heads-down to find out whatever I can about who they are and what they do."

It was ten o'clock that night when Angela came into Saxby's home office to find him rubbing his eyes at his desk. When he'd returned to the station with Sergeant

Barstow, he had gotten involved with several matters that needed his attention and that had taken up the rest of the day. After that, a relaxing dinner at home seemed like an idea too good to resist, even if he would have to follow it with a few hours of work.

"What can I get for you?" Angela said. "Or have you had enough for tonight? We could watch a show before bed if you want to unwind. How does that grab you?"

"That sounds good. I think I've had about enough for tonight," Saxby said. "I'll finish up with a few things in the morning, but I've got most of what I needed."

Angela pointed at one of the printouts on the desk. "Is that the wind farm company? The one that wants to build offshore?"

"Yep, that's them. Trans-Oceanic Wind," Saxby said. "I was trying to dig up whatever I could find on them. It's a French company but has large interests in Germany, the Netherlands, Belgium, and a bunch of other places. It's an old family company run by a lady named Claudine Bouchet, who I gather is the granddaughter of the founder."

"That's funny, because this says the full name of the company is Trans-Oceanic Wind & Son," Angela said, reading from the paper.

"That threw me for a minute too," Saxby said, "until I found an article that explained it. The 'son' was Claudine's older brother Phillipe, who died in an accident before he got old enough to take the helm of the company, which is how Claudine ended up in charge. The family uses the 'and son' on their letterhead as a way to honor Phillipe's memory."

"That's a sweet story," Angela said. "Come on out soon before you fall asleep at your desk and bang your head on the stapler."

"Will do, Ang," Saxby said. "I just need to print out a few more pages and I'm done for the night. Pour me a large glass of something good and I'll see you in a few."

21

The motor yacht *Flying Cloud* began her life as a typical mid-Atlantic commercial fishing boat, if large for her class at 125 feet from stem to stern, and almost 150 tons. Built and launched in Norfolk, Virginia, at the end of the '90's, she was moved up to Massachusetts, where she plied the Grand Banks for twenty years of longline tuna fishing before being purchased by Edward Batchelder, one of the heirs to the massive Batchelder Mining empire. "Batch," as his old buddies at Harvard had called him, proceeded to spend several million dollars having the *Flying Cloud* gutted and re-fitted as a luxurious seagoing yacht that he christened the *Bonnie Marie*. He told friends at the time that something about the lines of the boat appealed to him more than the ostentatious leisure boats the snobby Boston yacht brokers had been trying to sell him for years.

Fighting illness and finding himself spending more time than he liked helping to run the family business, he rarely had time to use the *Bonnie Marie*. Eventually, he sold it at a loss to a group of investors who had an idea for a small fleet of luxurious vessels they would rent out to well-heeled customers for a few days or weeks at a time. They guessed, correctly, that there was a substantial population of wealthy people who might enjoy the pampered life of cruising and living on a luxury yacht without the hassle and responsibility of actually owning a boat. Brewster Atwater, who had spent much of his life on or around boats, was one of those people. Like a grandparent who enjoyed playing with the young kids for a few hours and then was glad when the parents came to take them home, he relished being able to enjoy some time on a fine boat while leaving the logistics of running the thing to others.

At eight o'clock Saturday evening, the *Bonnie Marie* was cruising along at the leisurely pace of twelve knots. The seas were moderately rough, with swells around six feet, but the sky was clear and full of stars. The lights of Cape May, with Wildwood to the north, were small, bright specks in the distance to the west.

Inside, in the warm and clubby main salon, the crew had just cleared away the last remnants of dinner, and the six guests were considering their options for after-dinner drinks. As Brewster Atwater took his snifter of cognac to one of the overstuffed leather chairs that would have been at home in any high-end cigar lounge, Barry Vaughn and Jed Gatling stepped out to the promenade deck for a smoke.

"I don't like it, Jed. All just small talk so far," Vaughn said, "but it's gotta be one of them that messed with those scientists."

"To be fair," Gatling said, "it's got to be one of 'us.'"

Though, frankly, I don't think it's you and I know it's not me. It could be something else, right? Like robbery or who knows what else. I didn't even know those test tubers."

"Yeah, me either," Vaughn said. "I just hope the whole thing isn't blown. Maybe that's why Atwater brought us all here."

~

Several miles away, on the bridge of the Sentinel-class Coast Guard cutter *Flemington*, Captain Brian Ramsey had been going over plans with a guest.

"We're three miles out," Ramsey said. "Should be there in just a few minutes. You say the captain is a friend of yours?"

"Yes, an old friend from high school," Saxby said. "He's a master captain, certified for over a hundred tons. He's the captain, but he's still got the regular crew to drive the boat."

"How the hell did you manage to pull that off on such short notice?" Ramsey said.

"I sort of lucked out on that one," Saxby said. "When we started looking into the rental company that handles the *Bonnie Marie*, we saw that some of the crew overlapped with some of our Harbor House crews, covering days off, picking up extra shifts, that kind of thing. Once I knew that, it wasn't much trouble to pull in a favor or two and get my own guy in there as captain, on the condition that their regular team would actually run the *Bonnie Marie*."

A seaman came up and spoke briefly with Captain Ramsey.

"Okay, we'll be hailing them in just a few," Ramsey said. "You probably want to call your officers up, if they've packed in enough ginger ale. Like I told you, we'll get you over there, and the *Flemington* will give you the intimidation factor you wanted, but then I've got to make tracks up the coast. I'm leaving you in the capable hands of Lieutenant Lawson, along with two seamen—both armed, with the caveat that you return them to base in the same condition that you got them. Lastly, you'll have one of our fast response boats, which has a crew of six, including two divers, keeping an eye on you. It's the forty-five-footer just over there to port. Lieutenant Lawson will be able to communicate with them. They will report to him, and he will report to you while this action is underway. Sound good?"

On board the *Bonnie Marie*, Jed Gatling and Barry Vaughn had come back inside after their smoke break to join the others in the salon.

"It's strange, but it looks like there's a large ship out there that's about to pass really close," Vaughn said. "I almost think it might be Coast Guard."

At that moment, a man appeared in the salon, having come down the passageway from the direction of the bridge. He had a leather jacket slung over one arm. Atwater, who had arranged the cruise and paid the bill, was the first to speak:

"Captain, should we be worried about that ship coming so close to us?"

"That's what I came to tell you about," the captain said. "It looks like we're about to be boarded by the United States Coast Guard. That's the cutter *Flemington* approaching right now. They just radioed for us to stop engines and stand by to be boarded."

The guests looked all around at each other, exchanging looks of sudden confusion.

"Well, here they are," Vaughn said, watching out one of the salon windows. "They've stopped alongside us." Powerful floodlights mounted high up on the cutter suddenly flooded the stern deck of the *Bonnie Marie*. The bright light poured in through the salon windows.

"What the hell?" Gatling said. "Stand by to be boarded? I'm a U.S. citizen. Can they do that?"

"Yes, they can," the captain said. "They're the Coast Guard. They can pretty much board whoever they want to. I suggest we all just stay polite and cooperative and I'm sure it won't be any big deal. They probably just think we're someone we're not. I've got two of the crew lowering the stern stairs now, and if you'll excuse me, I'll go out and welcome our guests."

The captain pulled on his jacket and went out to the promenade deck, leaving the guests to talk amongst themselves. Atwater poured himself some more cognac and remained standing by the bar. For Gatling, it was a double bourbon whiskey. Barry Vaughn continued watching the activities outside on the stern deck. After about five minutes, a group of people approached the salon, led by the captain of the *Bonnie Marie*, who entered the salon first, followed by six others.

First of the six through the door were the three Coast

Guardsmen, clad in dark uniforms and tactical jackets. All three wore holstered pistols on their hips, while two of them held automatic rifles. They stepped to the left after entering to make room for the next three visitors. Chief Tate Saxby stepped inside, followed by Sergeant Barstow and Deputy Connor.

"Bloody hell, what is this?" Brewster Atwater said, coming towards Saxby, drink in hand. "This is a private party, and we've paid a lot for it. We aren't breaking any laws."

"I suspect you may be right that you're not breaking any laws at the moment," Saxby said, "but you see, we have a lot to talk about, and I didn't want to miss this opportunity to get you all together at the same time. I'm going to ask you all to just relax and I'm sure your questions will be answered. First, for those who don't know me, I am Chief Tate Saxby of the Cape May police. This is Sergeant Vicky Barstow, and Deputy Chase Connor. These three gentlemen here have escorted us over from the Coast Guard cutter *Flemington*, which will shortly be underway to its next appointment. Lieutenant Lawson?" Saxby gestured to Lawson.

"Yes, that's correct," Lawson said, "I am Lieutenant Lawson of the U.S. Coast Guard, and with me here are Seamen Garner and Smith. The *Flemington* has dropped us off here and will be on its way, but as you can see a hundred yards over to starboard is one of our fast response boats, with a crew of six, standing by to assist if needed. Captain Ramsey of the *Flemington* has placed us temporarily under the command of Chief Saxby, with orders to assist as needed."

"That's all very nice, but why are you here?" Jed Gatling said. "And by the way, we're on a ship at sea, so I'm not sure the Cape May police have any authority here. It sure doesn't seem like you're here with any kind of Coast Guard business. I mean, with respect to these officers."

"You know, he's right about that," Pearson said. "I own a fleet of fishing boats myself, and I know a little bit about maritime law. The captain has the authority here."

At that, the captain of the *Bonnie Marie* spoke up from across the room. "You're right there, Mr. Pearson. According to maritime law, the captain of a ship has wide ranging authority."

"And speaking of being the captain of this ship," Atwater said, coming up close to confront the captain. "You aren't even the regular captain that we've had before. Just who the hell are you anyway?"

"Cool your jets, man," the captain said, putting out his hands in a 'take it easy' gesture. "My name is Peter Hart, or Captain Peter Hart to you. I'm a fully licensed and certified master captain, and the legal captain of this boat today."

"What Pete didn't mention," Saxby said, "is that he and I have been friends since high school. I thought it would be good if he were to step in to captain the *Bonnie Marie* tonight, so I pulled a few strings and was able to make that happen."

"Well, if you're the captain," Atwater said, "who the hell is steering this boat right now?"

"All the regular people are running and steering the boat," Hart said. "There's nothing to worry about there. The people who served you dinner and set up the bar, the people who made up the cabins, all the regular crew. But tonight, I am the captain of this vessel, and as is my right under maritime law, I hereby cede my legal authority to the nearest civil police entity, which happens to be my old friend Chief Saxby here. I will retain command of the boat itself, of course."

All eyes in the room turned to Saxby, who had been moving slowly around the salon, stopping several times to sniff the air.

"Okay, I confess," Gatling said, theatrically. "I smoked a cigarette earlier. Don't tell me that's illegal on a ship at sea now."

"No, Mr. Gatling, it's not that," Saxby said. He looked slowly at each of the five guests in turn. "I've spoken with Mr. Atwater several times, and I met with Mr. Devere the other day. I'm already acquainted with Mr. Vaughn. I haven't yet met Mr. Rand Pearson—pleased to meet you Mr. Pearson. No, there's something else in the air here tonight, and, shall we say, 'the nose knows.'"

"Come on, Chief Saxby," Vaughn said. "What is the point of all this? We're all here for a relaxing cruise around the cape, I don't think there's any law against that."

"But is that really why you're all here, Mr. Vaughn?" Saxby said.

"What do you mean? Yes, that is why we're all here," Vaughn said.

"Okay. I'll get to the point shortly, don't worry," Saxby said. "But first, let me take a few minutes to tell you a story that I think you'll find interesting. Feel free to refill your glasses if you like, and get comfortable. I'll try not to bore you."

Lieutenant Lawson and the two seamen stood at ease

against the wall to one side of the door to the starboard promenade desk, watching intently, with Barstow and Connor on the other side. Captain Hart leaned against the wall near the door to the forward passage. Of the other five men, Atwater and Vaughn remained standing, while Pearson, Gatling, and Devere took seats and sipped their drinks. As Saxby spoke, he moved slowly around the salon.

"Something interesting happened to me last week when I first met with Mr. Atwater at his office. We talked for twenty minutes or so before I left, and when I got out to my car, I found myself suddenly flooded with memories of my late mother. Now, I've always been a somewhat sentimental person, and I miss my mother, so this in itself wasn't strange, but the timing was. I had just met with Mr. Atwater, and I was working on what appeared to be a murder case, which is not a happy thing. I didn't know why those memories came over me at that odd point in time. But it passed quickly and I went on with my day. Now bear with me, because I need to tell you a little bit about my mother."

"My God, is this really necessary?" Atwater said.

"Now, now, bear with me for a few minutes more," Saxby said. "I promise you that all will be revealed. Now, where was I? Oh yes—my mother grew up poor but proud in Dayton, Ohio. When she was nineteen or twenty, she did something that's been portrayed in countless books and movies. That is, she packed up and moved to New York City looking for work and a better life. Along with other jobs she held, she became an actual working model, mostly for catalogs and department store ads. It was nothing to get rich from, but one benefit was that she got to wear clothes and shoes she wouldn't otherwise have been able to afford, she got invited to fancy parties, and she got to have cocktails at places like the Waldorf or the St. Regis. Another thing was that she would sometimes get a sample, or a leftover tester bottle of an expensive and exotic perfume. That's how she fell in love with a certain ritzy perfume that became her signature scent. It was the scent of hers that I grew up with. As I got older and became able to buy her gifts with my own money, I would occasionally find a bottle of it for her, and she was always thrilled to have her old favorite. I miss her every day, but I'll never forget that scent. It's French, and it's called 'Ecusson,' by Jean D'Albert. Today, if you could even find it, it would probably cost hundreds of dollars. Certainly, a perfume for a wealthy lady with very refined tastes.

"Get on with it, get on with it—yeah, yeah, I know what you're all thinking. Now, the thing about this perfume is that I haven't smelled it for twenty years or more. That is, until last week. Since then, all of a sudden, I've smelled it not once, not twice, but *three times* within a matter of days."

"How good for you, Chief Saxby," Atwater said. "That sounds like a lovely story for the Hallmark Channel. Is there a point in this somewhere?"

"Patience, Mr. Atwater. We're getting there, full speed ahead," Saxby said. "Captain Hart, did you study the layout of this boat before you sailed earlier today?"

"Of course I did," Captain Hart said. "It's part of the captain's job to be familiar with the vessel."

"Then please tell me where these three doors lead to," Saxby said. He pointed to three doors in turn.

"This one right next to me is the main passage up to the

bridge and other forward parts of the boat," Captain Hart said. "That one there is to the catering kitchen, which is separate from the crew galley. The last one you pointed to is a combined butler's pantry and cloakroom."

"Thank you, Captain," Saxby said. "So, let's wrap up my story. The first time in twenty years that I've smelled Ecusson perfume, was last Wednesday afternoon at Mr. Atwater's office in Cape May. I got there just as he was showing his prior guest out, and I was introduced to a distinguished and expensively dressed lady by the name of Camille Duval. She seemed European to me, and in fact spoke with a pronounced German accent. We exchanged brief pleasantries and then she left, driving away in a dark blue Jaguar sportscar. It was only later that day that I realized she had been wearing my mother's old favorite perfume, which explains why those memories had popped up all of a sudden. The olfactory sense and memory have a very powerful linkage.

"The second time I smelled that same perfume was this past Monday, when I dropped in unannounced at the office of TOWSON Investments, in Sea Isle City. There were a few reasons I was interested in that firm, and I'll get to that a little later. As it turned out, the receptionist was the only person there, and she told me the manager had just left. But there it was in the lobby—a scent I'll never forget. And no, it wasn't the receptionist. I'm sure of that. I asked a few general investment questions and then left."

"So, you meet a lady at Brewster's office who wears a certain perfume," Vaughn said, "and then you smell the same perfume again at this investment place in Sea Isle. Even for a fancy perfume, that could still be a coincidence."

"You're right, Mr. Vaughn," Saxby said, "but given that the dark blue 2023 Jaguar F-Type that Camille Duval drove away from Mr. Atwater's office in is the same car that I saw leaving TOWSON Investments just as I arrived, makes me less inclined to think it could be a coincidence. In fact, since the Jaguar in question is registered to TOWSON Investments on Landis Avenue in Sea Isle City, I started to think that the Camille Duval I met in Cape May is also the missing manager of TOWSON Investments."

"You said there were three times that you'd recently smelled this perfume," Atwater said. "Are you going to tell us about the third?"

"The third time I smelled the perfume in a little over a week," Saxby said, "was about ten minutes ago, when I came into this room. There are other smells in here, to be sure, but my old nose is extremely sensitive, and rarely gets things wrong. That particular scent has deep meaning for me. Mr. Atwater, would you please open the cloakroom door over there and ask Miss Camille Duval to join us out here."

With a pronounced frown on his face, Atwater went over to the door and opened it. "You may as well come out and join us, Camille. It's more comfortable out here anyway."

Atwater stood aside as a lady emerged with an empty wine glass in her hand. She wore dark blue tailored slacks and black patent-leather loafers below a long-sleeved black cashmere sweater. Her chestnut hair was cut in a classic bob, and the only jewelry in evidence was a long, double strand of pearls. Saxby thought she looked to be about sixty, but knew her to be five years older than that.

"Well, this is good timing," she said. "I had run out of wine in there anyway. Nice to see you again, Chief Saxby."

"Likewise, Miss Duval," Saxby said. "Thanks for joining us. Please feel free to get yourself some more wine if you like. Have you been able to hear everything we've discussed so far?"

"Yes, loud and clear, as you Americans tend to say."

"Great. Well, now that we're all here," Saxby said, "we can—"

He was cut off by Jed Gatling, who had gotten up and come over close to him. "Yes, now that we're all here, Chief Saxby, what in hell is this all about?"

"Sit down please, Mr. Gatling," Saxby said. "I'm getting to that. Bear in mind that if one of you hadn't decided to hide in the cloakroom, we'd be ten minutes further along at this point.

"So, as I was saying, now that all *six* of you are here, I will tell you what I think you probably already know, and that is that we are here to talk about the murders of two of the scientists from the Cape Shore Marine Research Center of Cape May, and the related intrigue surrounding the work they were doing and how all of that might affect proposed plans to build a giant wind farm off the coast in this area. That, folks, is why we crashed your party tonight."

Saxby took a moment to look at all six of the guests in turn. Several of them stole quick glances at each other, while one stared intently at a spot on the carpet and another one looked straight ahead with a blank expression.

"First, let's talk a little bit more about TOWSON Investments and get something important out of the way.

"After having first bumped into Miss Duval last Wednesday, and realizing that the blue Jaguar was hers, I ran the plate, finding that it was registered to TOWSON Investments of Sea Isle City. Put a pin in that for a minute. Around this time, as I was investigating the death of the first of those scientists, Dr. Lewis Forbes, I kept hearing about these plans to build a wind farm, and who might be for it or against it. The company hoping to get the approval and the contract is a French company called Trans-Oceanic Wind. One day, when I was digging into that company to learn whatever I could about them, I learned that the full name of the company is actually Trans-Oceanic Wind *and Son*, and that's when it jumped out at me. Trans-Oceanic Wind and Son is *TOWSON*.

"After I realized that TOWSON Investments was a front for Trans-Oceanic Wind and Son, a French company, I started making a lot of calls, with help from Sergeant Barstow and Deputy Connor here. See, I may be just the police chief of small-town Cape May, but I have good friends I used to work with in the state police, and I also have friends in Homeland Security and in the State Department, and they have other overseas friends they can call. See how that works? So, anyway, I made a few calls and was able to find some very interesting information. In the end, now we know that Miss Duval here is the president of TOWSON Investments, and the four primary investors—through various cut-outs, naturally—are as follows: Brewster Atwater, Rand Pearson, Jed Gatling, and Bruce Devere. Sorry, Mr. Vaughn, I gather that you, as the youngest member of your group, came a little late to the party."

"Oh, you know me, Chief Saxby," Vaughn said, having walked over to the bar to refresh his brandy. "I've always believed it's fashionable to come in a little late."

"Yes, I might have heard that about you," Saxby said. "Moving on, there's one more thing I want to mention about TOWSON Investments and Trans-Oceanic Wind and Son, which are, for all intents and purposes, the same company. The current CEO of Trans-Oceanic Wind is a lady by the name of Claudine Bouchet. It took a bit of digging, but I was able to print out a recent picture from a charity event in Paris last year." Sergeant Barstow came up from behind Saxby to hand him some folded paper, which he took across to where Camille Duval was seated next to Brewster Atwater. "This first picture is from Camille Duval's New Jersey driver's license, and the other is of Trans-Oceanic Wind CEO Claudine Bouchet speaking with French actress Isabelle Huppert at that dinner in Paris." Saxby handed the papers to her. She looked at them briefly before handing them back.

"Well, now that we've settled that," Saxby said. "It would make things easier if I could just call you by your real name. Would that be acceptable to you, Madame Bouchet?"

"Yes, certainly that would be fine," Bouchet said. "And of course I'll be happy to pay any fines related to having a driver's license in a false name."

"We can talk about that another time," Saxby said. "Tonight, I'm here to talk about murder."

22

"Yes, that's right. I'm here tonight to talk about murder. Two murders, in fact," Saxby said. "It was a Monday morning, almost two weeks ago, that we found Dr. Lewis Forbes in his home, dead of an apparent assault. It looked like a confrontation that had gotten out of hand, or an argument that turned into a fight perhaps, as opposed to something premeditated. The first thing we did was to go through all the usual steps, soon ruling out robbery, drugs, a lover's triangle—none of that fit. It made sense then to look at his work at the research lab, where he had been part of a team looking at ways that certain marine animals—scallops, specifically—could be used to fight Alzheimer's disease. We soon realized that, if that research had been successful, it was very likely that some government entity would have taken steps to protect the scallop beds. We also realized that it was naïve to think that everyone would be thrilled to have this research be successful. Scallop fisherman could lose their access to the scallop beds, and the wind farm company wouldn't get to

build their wind farm, for example. We met with an aide to
Senator Charles Thackery, a known supporter of
Alzheimer's research. She confirmed for us that, if the
research being done here in Cape May was successful, the
senator would have done anything he could to kill the
wind farm project. We figured it was likely that contrac-
tors or realtors hoping to sell condos wouldn't want a
wind farm because, as I've learned, many people think the
windmills ruin the view. I met with a man last week who is
a well-known expert on renewable energy and all the argu-
ments for and against it, and he told me that I should be
looking at a group of people he called 'the power brokers.'
He told me, in essence, that, if you want to know who or
why someone would want to block a wind farm off South
Jersey, you need to talk to these people. I was initially skep-
tical of the idea of some kind of cabal, until I saw it myself.
I soon learned that yes, these five men are in *something*
together. *Up to something* together, you might say. Those
five men are now right here in this room. Five men who,
on the surface, would appear to be staunchly against the
idea of a big new wind farm off shore, for a number of
reasons. When Sergeant Barstow went to the office of
Tanner Construction to meet with Mr. Vaughn, she saw
Mr. Gatling and Mr. Atwater leaving. When I was at the
Oktoberfest event in Cape May on Saturday, I bumped
into Mr. Atwater and Mr. Devere. Remember that afternoon, Mr. Atwater? That was almost a week ago. That's
when you mentioned that you and Mr. Devere had just
been to a meeting in town. I did a little fishing, and I asked
you if it had been that meeting out at the Cape May Point
Science Center, and you said yes, it was. The funny thing

is, Mr. Atwater, that there was no such meeting on Saturday. There was nothing going on at the Science Center at all on that day. I think you were both probably at the informational wind energy presentation in the conference room at Congress Hall just before I ran into you a block away from there. That presentation, by the way, was sponsored by Trans-Oceanic Wind. That's the meeting you attended in town that day. I wonder if the rest of you were there too.

"Here's another puzzle. You five, one might think, represent groups you would initially expect to want the research to succeed, which is another way of saying you would not want the wind farm built. Yet, here you are clearly in some kind of partnership with Trans-Oceanic Wind. Here you are supporting and donating to TOWSON Investments, which is, of course, just a front for Trans-Oceanic Wind. It's a bit of a conundrum. Would you care to explain it to me, Mr. Atwater?"

"Well, it's what we talked about at my office last week," Atwater said. "If this wind farm doesn't get built, it'll be the next one, or the one after that. Bottom line is, the world is changing and you can only fight it for so long. I've spent much of my life in the fishing industry, in one capacity or other, along with Rand here. We've never been thrilled with the idea of offshore wind getting in the way of that. And Jed and Bruce had their own concerns for obvious reasons. For years, we've donated to candidates who shared our views and supported good legislation, but there's only so much you can do."

"As any sailor can tell you," Rand Pearson said, "when the wind changes and blows hard enough, you better adjust your sails or you might capsize."

"You've mentioned once or twice, Chief Saxby," Barry Vaughn said, "about the idea that people shopping for a shore house or condo might be put off by having to look out at a lot of windmills. That's been a real thing, no doubt, but our latest marketing research suggests that we've reached a tipping point on that. More and more people seem to think they're beautiful, or at least futuristic and cool-looking."

"So, what I think I'm hearing," Saxby said, "is that you noticed the change in the wind, as Mr. Pearson might say, and decided to throw in with Trans-Oceanic Wind in hopes that their wind farm project would go through."

"We like to make money, Chief Saxby," Atwater said. "So, we made adjustments. Not immediately, but after a year or more of poking it with a stick, that's what we did. We formed the TOWSON company and put a lot of money into it, trying to get support for the wind project."

"You also funded the research lab in Cape May, didn't you?" Saxby said. "That paper trail wasn't too hard to fox out, given that you are all legitimate philanthropists and there wasn't much need to hide your support. There wasn't anything illegal there. Of course, then we have to acknowledge what's strange about that. You were funding research into an effort to find ways that certain combinations of enzymes from Atlantic scallops could be used to treat Alzheimer's disease. Yet, if that effort was successful, such a finding would certainly be the death knell for the wind farm project. Remember what I said about Senator Thackery. He was a cheerleader for Alzheimer's research, but he also chaired the committee that would have decided if Trans-Oceanic Wind got the go-ahead for the project, and the huge federal grant that would go with it. Yet another puzzle there, isn't it?"

"The answer is simple, Saxby," Atwater said. "We funded the scallop research knowing it wasn't likely to go anywhere."

"In other words, you were putting on a show," Saxby said. "You were playing the good and generous citizens so that, when the research failed, probably within a few more months, you could come out smelling like roses, while still making an eventual killing when the wind farm project went through. Very clever. Oh ... I should add that the reason you knew the research would fail is that *one of you* had a close relationship with Dr. Arthur Hill, who had worked on similar projects during his prior tenure at a lab in Montauk."

Saxby looked directly at Bruce Devere as he mentioned Dr. Hill, noting how miserable he looked. Devere glared back at him.

"Yes, that's right, and I imagine you all know it already," Saxby said. "Dr. Hill spent years at a lab in Montauk, doing roughly the same work he picked up later here in Cape May. He's dead now, so we can't ask him about it, but I'll go ahead and assume that his more recent work was all with the best of intentions, despite the history of failure in Montauk. I've already established with Mr. Devere here that he and Dr. Hill knew each other back then, and maintained a friendly relationship for some years. Mr. Devere told me at his office a few days ago that he had not been in contact with Dr. Hill after he left the Montauk lab for Cape May, but that isn't true at all, is it, Mr. Devere?"

"Dammit, Bruce," Atwater said. "Don't tell me you—?"

Devere cut him off, yelling: "I just needed more time. It was happening too fast and I needed more time."

"I have no idea what the hell is going on here," Gatling said. "Can somebody tell me what's happening?"

"I certainly would like to know also," Madame Bouchet said. "Are we ever going to find out who killed those two scientists? Isn't that the root of why you're here, Chief Saxby?"

"Yes, Madame Bouchet, that is correct," Saxby said. He went to the bar to pour himself a coffee as he talked. "And now it's time for the last chapter of the story. Two killers have killed, and they themselves have been killed. But why? Mind you, I've had to fill in some blanks because … well, everyone's dead. Nevertheless, I'm quite confident that this is what happened.

"Two Sunday evenings ago, someone killed Dr. Lewis Forbes in his home. It took a few days of digging, and going through Forbes' papers and talking with various witnesses, but our investigation finally brought us to the point that we saw his co-worker, Dr. Arthur Hill, as the prime suspect. You see, on that Sunday evening at about ten-thirty, Hill went over to Forbes' house to talk with him, or confront him—convince him of something perhaps. The discussion got heated, and at some point, Hill picked up a blunt object and hit Forbes on the head. That might have been fatal in itself, but it didn't matter, because Forbes fell against a counter and broke his neck. But what was it that made Hill, who everyone thought was a calm and peaceful man, so angry? What made him so angry, ladies and gentlemen, was that he was in danger of losing everything.

"Early this year, Forbes, Hill, and the others weren't holding out much hope for the success of their scallop project. Someone who worked closely with both of them on the project told us they probably would have thrown in the towel within months. But then something changed and they started to see some more promising results. I gather that means they started to see more of the enzymes they were looking for, but I won't pretend to understand much about that. The point is that things started to look up. What had changed is that they had gotten in a new shipment of scallops. The research then continued with renewed energy, until after a few months, Forbes somehow determined that these latest scallops weren't from local waters at all. See, he knew about Hill's near success with the scallops from Long Island Sound years before. He acted on a hunch and quietly ordered a sample from a fishery in New London, soon confirming his suspicions that Hill had imported the latest scallops from that area in an attempt to skew the research."

"But why? Why would Hill have done that?" Atwater said.

"For enough money, is the short answer," Saxby said. "Because though Hill had made a good middle-class salary through his career, he saw an opportunity to finally make some really big money. Maybe not big to you people in this room, but big money to him. After he was killed, we went through all his stuff. Papers, finances, phone records—everything. One thing we found was a series of deposits, totaling about a hundred thousand dollars, to his account, from a company called 'Benthic Research,' which is owned by 'Paramount Legal Services,' which is owned by ...

DelVal United. And as we all know, the owner of DelVal United is Mr. Bruce Devere. The bigger thing, though, is the corporate bond that Hill had from DelVal United. If the company reached certain performance goals in the next three years, Hill stood to get a cool million. Do I have that about right, Mr. Devere?"

Devere, who had a hand covering most of his face, managed to croak out a response. "Alright. Enough. Yes. I paid him to find a way to keep the research going. Keep the project going. The whole scallop thing was his idea. I didn't know about that. I just needed more time, but I never meant for anyone to get hurt."

"That's right, you needed more time to liquidate some of your assets before the whole energy market on the East Coast changed," Saxby said. "Your PVC pipe company's been on the market for two years now, and the price has come down three times. Same with the tanker truck fleet in Bayonne. You paid him to find a way to give you more time to get out from under all that, but you didn't foresee Forbes finding out about the scheme. Hill tried to deal with that himself and we all know how that went. In the twenty-four hours after Hill killed Forbes, he called you six times from his cell phone. You must have had a challenge on your hands to try to talk him down after that."

"He told me it was an accident, and I believed him," Devere said. "He said he tried to convince the guy—Forbes —to keep quiet. Even offered him money, but he wouldn't go for it. He must have lost his temper."

"After that, Hill panicked and started calling you," Saxby said. "Over and over in fact. That's why, after a few days, you got a man named Jack Rhodes, who you knew from back on Long Island, to go down to Cape May, and ... what? Talk sense into Hill? Offer him still more money?"

"He was only supposed to scare the man," Devere said.

"Well, we have no way of knowing what their conversation was at this point," Saxby said. "But it must have gone from zero to sixty very fast, because Rhodes shot Hill in the head with a .38 caliber revolver. Are you sure that isn't what you sent him there to do?"

"No, of course not. I'm no mobster," Devere said. "I wouldn't even know how to ask for something like that. He was just supposed to make him shut up."

"Well, he sure did do that," Saxby said. "With a bullet to the back of the head, before trying to burn the place down and killing himself in the process. Where did you find this man, Jack Rhodes, Mr. Devere?"

"He was engaged to my niece, Julia," Devere said. "Used to be kind of a tough street punk, but he was trying to turn things around. He was the only person I could think of. My God—I shouldn't have gotten him involved. Now I find out Julia's pregnant—God, what have I done." Devere sat forward with his face in both hands, chest heaving and working to fight back tears.

"That's right, Mr. Devere," Saxby said. "A sad week for your family. Rhodes was engaged to your niece, which is why it was you and your attorney who arranged to have the body released so quickly. You must still have a few friends in high places."

At that moment, Captain Hart, who had left the salon ten minutes earlier, reappeared. "Pardon the interruption, folks, Chief Saxby. Just letting you know that a front has been moving in fairly quickly. Nothing to worry about at all, but the ride's going to get a little bit rougher out here, and I thought you should know why. Is it time to head back towards the harbor, Chief?"

"Maybe, Pete. How long would that take?"

"About thirty minutes."

"Okay, why don't we start back that way," Saxby said. He turned towards the Coast Guardsmen. "Lieutenant Lawson, would you please communicate to our escort out there that we'll be heading back to Cape May harbor."

The lieutenant walked to the rear of the salon to use his radio while Captain Hart went back up the passageway towards the bridge.

"You didn't have to do all of this, Bruce," Atwater said. "You could have talked to us. We could have figured something out."

Bruce Devere, still shaking but working to steady himself, stood up from the couch. "I need some fresh air. I'm just going to step out here for a few minutes." He walked unsteadily to the side door that opened out to the starboard promenade deck, bracing himself against the increasing sway of the boat.

"I'll keep an eye on him," Pearson said, following behind Devere and going out to lean against the rail next to the other man.

"What's going to happen to him now?" Atwater asked. "He's fighting some serious cancer. Probably doesn't even have a year left."

"He'll be charged with conspiracy to commit murder, among other things," Saxby said.

"It seems like that would be hard to prove, right?"

Gatling said. "You said it yourself, both killers are dead, and there doesn't seem to be a lot of evidence."

"I cannot disagree with you, Mr. Gatling," Saxby said. "It may be hard to prove, but I've spoken with the county prosecutor and that's what she wants to go for."

"Wait a minute," Atwater said, "you just said 'conspiracy to commit murder.' Surely you don't think the rest of us had anything to do with that?"

"Well, I'm no expert on the conspiracy laws," Saxby said, "but we've established that all of you were engaged in an effort to influence the government's decision about the wind farm, and you've admitted to forming a shell corporation using a series of cutouts as part of that effort. If only one of you—Mr. Devere—took steps that eventually led to the murders of Forbes and Hill, but it was *in furtherance of that overall effort*, well, that just might meet the criteria for conspiracy."

"That's just crazy. That's really a stretch," Gatling said. "They'll never prove conspiracy for something like that."

"You might be right, Mr. Gatling," Saxby said. "But the other thing you're all going to be charged with will be easier to prove. I'm speaking of conspiracy to use false information or processes to unfairly influence the federal grant system."

"That's another charge that's going to be hard to prove," Atwater said. "I think your prosecutor might just be grasping at straws."

"You might be right also, Mr. Atwater," Saxby said. "But that's all up to the prosecutor and maybe the jury to decide. The third charge, though, might be the kicker. I think that could be the one that makes you all write some big checks and spend some time as guests of Club Fed. That's the same charge as the last one, but with a bonus—conspiracy to use false information and processes to unfairly influence the federal grant system *while colluding with a foreign national*.

"There we have, I'm quite sure, the reason you went to so much trouble to keep your connection to Madame Bouchet a secret. Perhaps the reason that she first spoke to me with a pronounced German accent, and also why she tried to hide in the cloakroom when we first came aboard. Your efforts to influence the federal grant process are one thing, but involving a French citizen is, as some might say, 'a whole 'nother thing.'"

The turning motion of the boat could be clearly felt as Rand Pearson came back in from where he'd been standing outside with Devere. He stepped carefully to account for the rising and falling of the deck. "I just came in to get us both a drink. I hope I haven't missed anything exciting."

Barry Vaughn yelled out suddenly, leaping to his feet while pointing at the salon door that Pearson had failed to fully latch. "He's trying to go over the rail!"

After no more than one or two seconds of shock, several people in the salon, including the Coast Guardsmen, started to move. Vaughn, who was closest to the door at that moment, was in the lead. "C'mon, Bruce, don't do that," he yelled. As he launched himself through the door, the deck suddenly rose, causing him to catch his foot on the storm threshold and sprawl almost horizontally across the teak walkway outside. The last thing Vaughn saw before his head smashed into one of the galvanized steel rail supports was Bruce Devere going over the side into the black water below.

23

A lot happened fast.

Lieutenant Lawson yelled into his radio for the fast response boat to close in and get a diver in the water, while at the same time one of the Coast Guardsmen started sweeping the water along the side of the boat with a powerful flashlight.

The second Coast Guardsman, along with Sergeant Barstow, checked out Barry Vaughn, who was bleeding profusely from the skull, and appeared unresponsive.

Saxby grabbed Deputy Connor by the arm. "I don't know how to call the captain. See if you can find the bridge as fast as you can and tell them *man overboard*. We need to stop this boat." Connor nodded and took off through the front passageway.

Claudine Bouchet came through the door to kneel alongside Barstow at Vaughn's side. "Let me help. I got halfway through medical school a long time ago." She started to look Vaughn over, examining the wound on his forehead before checking for a pulse.

It was a few minutes before Barstow came back inside to speak with Saxby. "That other boat's got two divers in the water back about a hundred yards behind us, looking for Devere. I don't think they've got anything yet."

"Jesus, what a mess," Saxby said. "What about Vaughn? What's his condition?"

"Vaughn's dead, Chief," Barstow said. "Instantly is my guess. His head hit that steel support like a battering ram. The French lady checked him out too. She has some medical school."

"Man, that's horrible," Saxby said. "I'll give the guy some credit. He died trying to stop Devere from killing himself."

Lieutenant Lawson interrupted them, coming in with flashlight in hand. "They got him, Chief. He drowned, but at least we've recovered the body."

"Okay, thank you, Lieutenant. That's some good, fast work by you and your team," Saxby said. "That's two dead now, since Mr. Vaughn bashed his head. I'm going to tell Pete to get us back into port on the double."

The lieutenant went back outside and Saxby turned to face the remaining guests. Bouchet was just coming out of the restroom, having gone in to wash Vaughn's blood from her hands. She went over to the bar and poured herself a triple brandy from a crystal carafe before joining Atwater on the leather settee. Pearson and Gatling stood together near the billiard table.

"It looks like the body count now stands at five," Gatling said. "What happens now?"

"We are headed into port," Saxby said, "where the four of you will be arrested on the charges I described earlier. It's obviously late at night, so I think we can arrange to have you spend the night in your cabins here on the *Bonnie Marie* rather than in the city holding cells. Under guard, of course. You'll be arraigned in the morning at the county court, and then the wheels of justice will start to turn. Slowly, most likely, but they will turn. I'd be surprised if you weren't all released on bail, but that's not up to me."

24

I t was several days after the adventure on the *Bonnie Marie*, and Saxby was finishing up a quick chat with Officer Megan Hayward at the station.

"I'll let you get back to work, Megan, but I just wanted to be sure to thank you personally for all the good work you've done over the past couple of weeks while I was focused on this crazy wind farm case. Vic, Three, and I were only able to do what we needed to do because we knew you and the others were holding down the fort and handling all the other stuff. Those fender benders, the shoplifting, the late-night drunks, all that still needs to be handled professionally, and we count on you folks for that. So, thank you."

Saxby had been making it a point to catch up with all of the junior officers for similar conversations over the past few days, with Hayward being the last. After an hour of paperwork at his desk, he was thinking of walking down to Starla's Café for a sandwich, when Barstow stuck her head into his office.

"Have you heard back from the prosecutor's office yet, Chief?"

"Yes, and as a matter of fact I just finished reading her email," Saxby said. "Care to join me for lunch at Starla's and I'll tell you about it?"

Five minutes later, with coats on, they set out for the few-block walk.

"Actually, there isn't much to tell," Saxby said, "and no big surprises. She's decided to drop the conspiracy to commit murder charge against the four of them. It's her call but I have to agree. There really isn't any evidence linking the rest of them to that part of it, and also, I'm pretty sure she thinks that all the people who really were involved are now dead, in one way or another. That'll save the taxpayers some money. We don't have concrete evidence that Hill killed Forbes, but the mountain of circumstantial is enough for the prosecutor. Clearly, that's what happened."

"I gotta say, it makes sense," Barstow said. "Everyone who killed someone, or hired somebody to threaten someone, has been killed, along with the top guy, Devere. Wrapped up kinda neatly if you think about it. I guess you could say that justice was done all around. It's such a shame about Lewis Forbes. Out of the five dead, he was the only true innocent. Crazy how the world works sometimes. What about the other charges for those 'power broker' people?"

"The charges have all been filed as expected," Saxby said. "And they've been released on their own recognizance. Again, no surprise there. Claudine Bouchet has left the country already. I guess they've got something on her to make her come back. They'll all probably just get hefty fines, but they certainly aren't going to get their wind farm built."

"Alright, well, at least they'll get something. Money is what they care about the most, and that's where they'll get hit," Barstow said. "By the way, when you asked me to look into the *Bonnie Marie*, you never did tell me what led you to that. How did you know they'd all be there on that boat?"

"Oh, that was just logical deduction based on dumb luck, I guess," Saxby said. "When I was in Devere's office up on Route 9, I noticed a brochure for the *Bonnie Marie* on his desk. It had a sticky note on it, which I couldn't read, but I took a guess and figured it might be a date and time. He had just told me that he was leaving town the next day but would be back for a 'get-together' by the weekend. It made sense to me that a boat rental like that would be a good way for the six of them to get together away from any prying eyes. That's all. Nothing worthy of Sherlock Holmes."

"Well, you were right on there, Chief," Barstow said. "Sherlock Holmes or not, that was a good move. And wow, how about Barry Vaughn? What do you think about all that?"

"Yeah, Barry Vaughn, that's really something, isn't it?" Saxby said. They walked in silence for a moment before he spoke again. "The good ... they die young."

It was the Saturday of the following weekend that Saxby did something highly unusual: he took a whole day off work. He and Angela put together a small picnic of take-out sandwiches, chips, a few cookies, and two bottles of wine, taking it out to the beach at Cape May Point.

They wore jeans and chunky sweaters and sat in low beach chairs with the food and wine set out on a portable little table between them. The mid-October weather was seasonably mild, at about sixty degrees with a light breeze. There was a sparse scattering of other people on the beach, including a few couples indulging in their own personal picnics. Dog walkers and their dogs passed by every now and then.

"I ran into Vic at the Acme the other day," Angela said. "She was telling me how great you did out on that boat. She said it was like something from a movie."

Saxby laughed at that while pouring wine into a plastic cup, causing him to spill a little. "Well, that's nice of her to put it that way. I can see how it might have looked like that. Like a movie sure, but unfortunately some parts were like a horror movie."

"I heard some people talking in the bar the other day," Angela said, "about how you were becoming well known around the state as some kind of great detective. Are you going to take that guy from the *New York Times* up on his idea for an interview?"

"Ugh, I guess I have to decide about that, don't I?" Saxby said. "I don't see why not, as long as it's okay with the mayor."

After a while, a couple passed close by, stopping for a friendly exchange about the weather and how nice it was to be able to walk on the beach at this time of year. They asked about favorite restaurants and Angela gave them some ideas, along with an invitation to come by the Ugly Mug to join them for a drink on the house later.

"Thanks, we'll probably take you up on that," the man said. They started to turn away. "Appreciate the recommendations and we'll let you get back to your picnic. Maybe we'll see you later. Oh hey, be careful with that wine on the beach, I saw a cop car parked just over there."

"Thanks, but I think it'll be fine," Angela said. "I'm in good with the chief of police"

"They seemed nice," she said, as the strollers continued their walk down the beach. "But you heard what he said— be careful with that wine. We don't want to get in any trouble with the law. I hear they're pretty tough around these parts."

"Ang, as I'm sure I've told you before," Saxby said, holding up two half-full wine bottles, "I *am* the chief of police, and I say... red or white?"

ACKNOWLEDGMENTS

As with all my other books, I could not have completed Windy With a Chance of Murder without the assistance of several people. For their important work as beta readers for this project, I owe a huge thank you to my wife Bonnie Boumiea, along with friends and neighbors Dr. Judy Ozment and Shari Glaskin. Along with helping with some initial editing, beta readers have the critical responsibility to give a writer their first impressions of a piece of work. Does the story make sense? Does the pacing keep you interested? Do you believe the characters would do what they do? When a chapter ends, do you wish you had time to read the next one? These people are empowered to 'tell it to me straight', and their feedback is critical to the process. The person who worked the hardest on this book (I mean, you know, aside from me), is my wife Bonnie. A huge thank you to her for her long hours spent on several read-throughs, including the final line-by-line very close read. Thanks for being there for me BB.

A big thank you also to Lee Burton of Ocean's Edge Editing up there in Canada. Lee has worked with me on several of my books, and his help is much appreciated.

A note on wind farms and wind energy in general: I realize that this can be something of a political football to many people, but to me, I chose the topic just because the potentially huge money involved in these kinds of projects seemed like good material for a murder mystery. It is my hope that I've been able to weave together a fun and interesting story without shoving a pro or con agenda in anyone's face. Thanks to Mark Allen (who is a real person, by the way), for the initial germ of the idea.

ABOUT THE AUTHOR

Miles Nelson spent thirty years with a Fortune 500 company before moving on to other pursuits. A New Jersey native who grew up in Cape May, he has traveled extensively across the U.S., as well as to Europe and to numerous Caribbean and Bahama islands. When not writing or traveling, he enjoys cooking, photography, guitar playing, watching movies, and trying new wines. He lives in the Philadelphia suburbs with his wife Bonnie and their cat Starla. *Windy With a Chance of Murder* is his sixth novel and is the fourth Cape May murder mystery. For more information, go to www.milesnelsonauthor.com, or to the Facebook page "Miles Nelson Author".

ALSO BY MILES NELSON

The Privilege of The Dead (2018)

To Die No More (2019)

Murder at Exit 0 (2020)

Murder is a SHORE Thing (2022)

Death Rents a Beach House (2023)